ARTHUR AND KIP

By Clotilde Zehnder

SAVAGE MOUNTAIN PRESS

For Hans and Ephrem

Contents

1

Arthur

Miss Rachel was vigorously sweeping her front porch one fine spring day. Miss Rachel swept her front porch every day the weather permitted, and when the weather was particularly nice she was particularly vigorous. She liked her porch to be clean, as she liked everything to be clean, and it was a good way to watch the goings-on in Nightingale Lane. Miss Rachel's house stood at the top of the street, giving her an excellent vantage point from which to watch those goings-on.

Miss Rachel wore plain, no-nonsense skirts and blouses, and her hair was always twisted up in a tight knot on the back of her head. This, combined with the neatness of her house and lawn, gave her an air of severity. But, despite all appearances, everyone on Nightingale Lane knew Miss Rachel to be a kind, warm-hearted woman who loved children. The children of Nightingale Lane loved to

1

come and play on her lawn, and she always had a cookie jar full of the most excellent cookies.

Miss Rachel looked out over the peaceful neighborhood. Nightingale Lane was a wide cul-de-sac with nine houses, each with spacious lawns. It was a very old neighborhood, built over the past several hundred years. It was just the right size to keep an eye and a finger on all the goings-on. Everyone in Nightingale Lane knew everyone else, and everyone was most friendly to everyone else.

"Why, it's Tot Feet," said Miss Rachel, as a child came up to her front porch. The child thus addressed, a boy of eight years with unruly brown hair, brown eyes, and an impudent nose, smiled sweetly at Miss Rachel. Tot Feet was what Miss Rachel called Arthur Ramsay, short for Terror on Two Feet. Arthur was known all over Nightingale Lane by that name, though he had lived there for no more than two weeks.

Arthur sat on Miss Rachel's porch railing and kicked his feet happily. "Why the blissful expression?" asked Miss Rachel.

"Lydia said I had to stay in the house all morning because I broke her favorite tea cup, but I only had to stay in for an hour. Lydia told me to go out and not come in until lunch time because I was driving her up a wall. I wonder why people say that. I don't think anyone could actually drive up a wall."

"You seem very proud of that fact," said Miss Rachel.

"Mmhmm," Arthur said contentedly.

"You *are* a terror on two feet, and no denying it," Miss Rachel said.

Arthur smiled angelically. Why was it that naughty children had angelic smiles? Miss Rachel wondered to herself. Really good children often had horrid, priggish smiles; nice children had nice smiles; but naughty children had angelic smiles.

"Can I have a cookie?" Arthur asked.

"May I." Miss Rachel considered it her duty to help bring up the children of Nightingale Lane properly. "Would Lydia want you to have one?"

"Probably not."

"Then perhaps you shouldn't have one."

"Why?"

"Well, if Lydia's already mad at you, you wouldn't want to make her angrier, would you?"

Arthur considered this. "She needn't know," he said at last.

Miss Rachel swatted him with her broom. "Get along with you," she said cheerfully. "Dennis should take a stick to you more often."

"What'll he do with it after he takes it to me?" Arthur said impudently. "*I* wouldn't want any old stick."

"You!" Miss Rachel made a gesture with her broom, and Arthur ran off, laughing.

Miss Rachel smiled to herself and went back to sweeping her porch. Her cousin Maria was coming up the

3

street, and she couldn't have a dirty porch with Maria around. Maria did talk so…

Dennis Ramsay turned onto Nightingale Lane and was nearly knocked over by a small figure catapulting through the air. Dennis grabbed the shoulders of the small figure and said, "Slow down, Arthur. You'll knock someone over if you keep doing that."

"Oh, I did already," said Arthur. "It was Mr. Cameron."

"Arthur!" Dennis groaned. "I hope you said you were sorry."

Arthur thought about it. "I think I did."

They passed Miss Rachel's house. She was sitting on her porch, drinking tea and chatting with her cousin Maria. Miss Rachel waved at Dennis and Arthur, and they waved back.

"Dennis Ramsay, your brother is a tribulation come to life," Miss Rachel called.

"Don't I know it!" Dennis called back, and tipped his hat to the two ladies.

"Who was that?" asked Cousin Maria when the Ramsays had gone on.

"The Ramsays," answered Miss Rachel. "The older one is Dennis. He and his wife Lydia live in the old Henderson house. Old Charlie Henderson was their great-uncle. Dennis is the new doctor at the hospital."

"He doesn't look old enough to be the boy's father," Cousin Maria said.

"He isn't. The boy is Dennis' little brother, Arthur. Their parents died about five years ago, and Dennis has practically raised Arthur. Arthur is a terror. We call him the Terror on Two Feet, or Tot Feet for short." Miss Rachel knew the histories of everyone on Nightingale Lane, no matter how long or how short of a time they had lived there.

"I see," said Cousin Maria disapprovingly. Cousin Maria seldom approved of anything.

Lydia seemed more cheerful at lunch. She had made a blueberry cake for dessert, and she did not tell Dennis that Arthur had broken her teacup. Arthur was very relieved. Dennis could be very stern when Arthur made trouble for Lydia.

During dessert, Dennis was telling Lydia about something someone had said at the hospital when he saw a curious sight. Arthur had his napkin tied across his nose and mouth and he was very carefully cutting up his slice of cake with two knives, taking the blueberries out and putting them to one side. "What on earth are you doing?" Dennis asked.

"I'm dissecting my cake," Arthur answered, his voice slightly muffled by the napkin.

"Eat your cake properly, or you can't have any," Dennis ordered, trying hard not to smile. It didn't do to encourage Arthur, he had learned very early on.

5

"How can I be a doctor when I grow up if I don't practice dissecting?" Arthur asked as he untied the napkin.

"Dissecting cake won't give you practice, and besides, doctors don't dissect anymore," said Dennis.

Grownups were no fun, Arthur thought. They didn't let you do anything. Maybe he would not be a doctor when he grew up. It was no fun if there was no dissecting involved. What was the point of being a doctor if you couldn't dissect? Maybe he would be a pilot. He would like that; it must be very exciting to fly. Lydia would probably say it was too dangerous, though. He sighed and popped the rest of his cake into his mouth. "Can I have some more?" he asked around his mouthful.

"May I," corrected Lydia.

"May I," said Arthur.

Lydia served him another piece of cake, and gave one to Dennis. "Delicious cake," Dennis said, smiling at her. Lydia beamed. She had not started out as a good cook, but now, after being married to Dennis for a year and a half, she could cook almost anything.

Dennis finished his cake and glanced at his watch. "I have to be back at the hospital early today. Goodbye, Lydia. Behave yourself now, Arthur." He kissed Lydia, rumpled Arthur's hair, and left.

Arthur cleared the table, for that was his job, then went outside before Lydia could tell him to clean up his room. He wandered down the street, daydreaming about being a pilot. It did sound much better than being a doctor.

Besides, Dennis said that to be a doctor you had to be very good at school work, especially math and science, which Arthur didn't really care for.

Nightingale Lane was empty; even Miss Rachel was not on her porch. At that time of day people were either finishing lunch or resting. Miss Rachel would not be resting. She was probably cleaning. Miss Rachel was obsessed with cleaning, Arthur thought. Why anyone would *want* to be clean was beyond him, and why anyone would take pains to be clean was out of reach. He would hate to live with Miss Rachel, even though she made the best cookies. Living with Lydia was bad enough. Living with Miss Rachel was unthinkable. He shivered dramatically at the thought. He would soon have no skin left if he lived with her, for she would be always washing it.

"Arthur! Arthur Ramsay!" called an imperious voice. He looked up. Angel Lidden was standing at the fence in front of her house. He stopped and looked at her. Angel was snooty as the day was long. She was dressed in a spotless white lace dress, and her golden curls were carefully brushed and tied back with a blue ribbon. To most adults she was cute and charming. To Arthur she exuded pure evil.

"What?" he said, more rudely than not.

"Mommy doesn't like you. She says you're a bad boy. Are you a bad boy?"

Arthur shrugged.

"She says you're not nice either," Angel continued. "I don't think you're nice. Nice people don't shrug their shoulders like that."

Arthur shrugged again and began to saunter off. Angel was not to be defeated like that, though. She was used to having her own way. "It's a good thing Miss Lydia's married to your brother," she said. "Otherwise there would be no one to take care of you. No one would want to."

Arthur did not say anything to that. He waited till Angel had grown tired of watching his retreating back, and then he looked around him for ammunition. There was a nice big patch of mud at the edge of Mr. Cameron's lawn. Arthur scooped up two large handfuls, and ran back to Angel's house. Angel had just turned away from the fence and was making her way to the porch, and her back was to him. Arthur pulled back his hand and let fly one lump of mud. *Splat!* It landed with a satisfying sound squarely on the back of Angel's head, covering her perfect golden curls. She turned around with a cry of anger and dismay, and Arthur let fly his second handful of mud. This one landed smack dab in the middle of her spotless white dress, leaving a huge brown spot.

Angel started to scream. Mrs. Lidden came running out of her house, and started to yell at Arthur. People poked their heads out of doors and windows. Arthur beat a quick retreat. He would probably get in big trouble for throwing mud at Angel Lidden, he knew, but it had been terribly satisfying all the same.

Lydia caught him as he was sneaking into the house before dinner. "Arthur Ramsay," she said, "Mrs. Lidden just called."

"Oh," said Arthur.

"She's very angry about what you did to her daughter. Go up to your room until Dennis gets home."

Arthur walked slowly up to his room, where he set about drawing pictures of the demise of Angel Lidden, all of which were painful and gory.

Dennis came up just before dinner and stood in the doorway of Arthur's room with his hands in his pockets. "Lydia just told me about your doings this afternoon," he said. "It never is an uneventful day for you, is it? Mrs. Lidden's very angry. Whatever possessed you to throw mud at Angel? Oh never mind; I don't think I really want to know."

"She was being nasty," Arthur said. "And she's so stupid."

"That's not a kind thing to say, even if she was being nasty," Dennis said. "And it was wrong of you to throw mud at her. I'm ashamed of you, Arthur. After dinner we will go over and you will apologize to Angel, and then you will stay in your room for the rest of the evening."

"Dennis!" Arthur wailed. "That's not fair!"

"It most certainly is fair," Dennis said. "You can't go around throwing things at people, especially girls, just because they say nasty things. It's not gentlemanly."

"I'd rather not be a gentleman then," Arthur grumbled.

"Perhaps not, but for now you must try. Come on down now; it's time for dinner."

Arthur heaved a heavy sigh and followed his brother downstairs.

After dinner Arthur and Dennis set out for the Liddens' house. Mrs. Lidden answered Dennis' knock. "Mrs. Lidden, I'm Arthur's brother, Dennis Ramsay," Dennis said. "Arthur has come to apologize to Angel."

"Come in," Mrs. Lidden said, smiling at Dennis and glaring at Arthur.

The next afternoon, Arthur went out after lunch, and passing by the Liddens' house, he stopped for a moment and stood surveying it. Mrs. Lidden came out of the front door and called out, "Arthur Ramsay, you stay away from my Angel, you hear me?"

"You don't have to keep telling me that, you know," Arthur said. "I still hate Angel, but I'm not going to do anything to her."

Mrs. Lidden was so stunned by his impudence that she could not say a word. She gaped, her mouth hanging open like a fish. At last she managed to say, "Your brother will hear of this," and flounced into her house.

Arthur was not worried. He sauntered down the street. When he reached Miss Rachel's house, she was on the front porch sweeping, as usual. Arthur said, "Dennis wasn't mad at me for breaking Lydia's cup."

"He wasn't?" Miss Rachel looked questioningly at Arthur. "That's strange."

"Lydia didn't tell 'im. But Mrs. Lidden's mad at me."

"Did you bother Angel again?"

"No, but I said I hated Angel, and I guess that made her mad. Angel's so stupid. She has a stupid name, too."

"Well, no child should have to live up to such a name," said Miss Rachel, "and no decent Christian should call her child Angel. But you shouldn't go around insulting people."

Arthur shrugged. "Well, I'm going to take a walk," he said complacently. "Oh, I'm going to be a pilot when I grow up, not a doctor."

"If you were born to walk the ground, remain there; do not fool around," quoted Miss Rachel. "Airplanes are dangerous things. Take my advice and stay away from them."

"There's no dirt in the air," Arthur said, and skipped away, leaving Miss Rachel to look after him, shaking her head in bewilderment.

2

Arthur and Kip

Arthur loved his new home. The house had belonged to his and Dennis' great-uncle, Charles Henderson, who had left it to Dennis when he died. He had always been fond of the Ramsays and had been known to say that they were the only decent people in his extended family. The Ramsays had been living in a little apartment in the city, and Arthur had absolutely detested it. The city was an awful place to live. There was hardly any place to play. It was very lucky that Great-Uncle Charles had died, Arthur thought. Well, not that he had died, though he was very old, but that he had left them the house on Nightingale Lane.

Arthur loved the big old house, full of old and interesting things, including a secret passage and a hidden room, but most of all he loved the yard. Great-Uncle Charles had not been able to keep it up much, so it was rather overgrown. Dennis and Lydia were trying to make it look nice and tidy again, but Arthur thought it was perfect the way it was. He had numerous hide-aways, and there were plenty of good climbing trees, which was evident from his torn trousers and skinned knees.

Next to the Ramsays' house was another one, and its yard and the Ramsays' were not visibly separated, since there was no fence. The only thing that divided the two yards was a big old tree. The house next door was empty at the moment; the owners were away on vacation, Miss Rachel said. It was also a nice house – all the houses on Nightingale Lane were nice houses – but not as nice as Arthur's, at least in his own opinion. Between the Ramsay's lawn and that of the house next door there was a very good climbing tree. It was Arthur's favorite tree, and he claimed it as his own. Arthur had been living in Nightingale Lane for no more than a few weeks when he found an intruder. He was walking under his favorite tree, intent on climbing it, when he looked up and saw two legs hanging down from a limb. They were covered in dark blue cloth and ended in a pair of rather dirty feet. The top half of the intruder was hidden by leafy boughs. Rage filled Arthur. How dare anyone climb his tree? He picked up a rock and threw it at the legs.

"Ow!" said the owner of the legs.

"Get out of my tree!" Arthur commanded.

"How do you know it's your tree?" was the impertinent answer.

"I found it first!" Arthur said. "Finders keepers."

"It was mine first," the intruder said. "I've lived here longer than you have. You've just come, haven't you? Mr. Henderson lived here."

"I'm his great-nephew," Arthur said. "I'm sure he lived here longer than you did."

He of the blue-clad legs seemed unable to dispute this claim. The legs disappeared, and a moment later a boy landed on the ground beside Arthur. He looked to be about Arthur's own age, and he had a very untidy mop of curly red hair and a million freckles. He stuck out his hand. "I'm Kip Mortimer," he said.

Arthur shook his hand. "What sort of name is Kip?" he asked.

"My real name's Christopher-Paul, after my father's father and my mother's father," the boy said. "But no one ever calls me that, because it's too long, especially if you add Mortimer at the end, except for my mother when she's mad at me. What's your name?"

"Arthur Ramsay," Arthur said. "We moved in here three weeks ago."

"We've been on vacation," Kip said. "We've just come back. My father is the principal at my school. What does your father do?"

"I don't have a father," Arthur answered. "My brother's a doctor at the hospital."

"Oh," said Kip. "Let's be friends."

"All right," said Arthur. "Let's climb the tree."

14

When lunch time came, Kip suggested that Arthur come to his house for lunch. "All right," Arthur said. "I have to ask Lydia."

"Who's Lydia?" asked Kip.

"She's my sister-in-law, because she's married to my brother," Arthur explained. He was very knowledgeable about these things.

"Oh," said Kip.

They ran inside, where Lydia was starting lunch. "Who's this?" she asked. "A new friend, Arthur?"

"This is Kip Mortimer," Arthur explained in a rush, "an' he lives next door, an' he wants me to come to his house for lunch. Can I?"

"Well, very nice to meet you, Kip Mortimer," Lydia said. "So you're back from vacation?"

"Yes, ma'am," Kip said, holding out his hand. "How d'you do?"

Lydia raised her eyebrows. "My, what nice manners. Do you see that, Arthur?" She smiled at Kip.

"Can Arthur come to my house for lunch?" Kip asked.

"Will your mother mind?" Lydia asked.

"No, she won't," Kip said. "She likes to have people over. Please, can Arthur come?"

"All right," Lydia said. "Tell your mother I will come and visit her soon."

"I will," Kip said. "Thank you, Mrs. Ramsay. It was nice to meet you."

Dennis came in at that moment. He took off his hat and hung it up. "Oh, I see that we have a visitor," he said. "I heard someone being polite, and I thought I had forgotten to wake up this morning, and it was Arthur."

Arthur made a face and Dennis ruffled his hair.

"Dennis, do you know Kip Mortimer?" Lydia asked. "He belongs to the family that lives next door. They've just come back from vacation."

"Yes, Kip and I met this morning on my way to the hospital," Dennis said.

"Arthur's coming to my house for lunch," Kip said.

"Well, have a good time, boys." Dennis went to kiss Lydia, and the boys scurried away, Kip because he was anxious to bring Arthur to his house, and Arthur because he was always disgusted when Dennis and Lydia kissed. He never could understand why married people had to kiss each other. Why couldn't they just shake hands like normal people?

Kip's house was a nice one, although it was not as nice as Arthur's. No house was as nice as Arthur's, in his opinion. Kip had a mother and a father, though. Kip's father was not home, but his mother was, and she was pretty, Arthur thought. Very much what his own mother would have been like. Arthur had seen many pictures of his mother, but in his head she was always different from the photographs in the big album in the living room. It was hard to keep photographs in your head.

Kip's mother was making lunch when the boys came in. "Why, who's this?" she asked, wiping her hands on her apron.

"This is Arthur Ramsay," Kip explained. "He lives next door. I invited him to lunch."

"Well, that's very kind of you," Kip's mother said. "It's very nice to meet you, Arthur. I will have to go over and visit your mother soon."

"I don't have a mother," Arthur said. "I have a sister-in-law. She's married to my brother. I live with them."

"Oh," said Kip's mother in a funny voice. She put her arm around Arthur. "Well, I'll have to visit your sister-in-law then. I'm glad someone moved into the old house next door. It's been very empty since Mr. Henderson went into the hospital two years ago. Well, boys, I have sandwiches and lemonade for lunch, and you can have some cookies afterwards. How does that sound?"

"Yum," said Kip.

"I suppose you haven't met Kip's older brother and sister," Kip's mother said. "They're out with friends at the moment, but I'm sure you'll meet them soon."

"Oh, you don't need to," Kip said. "They're nothing special."

"Kip!" said his mother. "All right, boys, lunch is ready."

Kip and Arthur sat down at the kitchen table, and Kip's mother served them lemonade and ham and cheese sandwiches cut into star shapes. Arthur wished Lydia would cut his sandwiches into star shapes. But perhaps she did not know how. He would have to remember to tell her to ask Kip's mother how to do it. The boys ate hungrily, and the sandwiches were gone in no time. Then they ate their cookies – chocolate chip – with milk, and Kip's mother suggested that Kip show Arthur the house and the yard.

Kip's house was old and big, though not as old and big as Arthur's, and there was no secret passage or hidden room. But it was a nice house all the same. Kip had a big collection of wooden soldiers complete with cannons and other such articles of war. The boys forgot about the outdoors and settled down to play with the wooden soldiers. Arthur was the blue side, and Kip was the red side. They staged a fearsome battle on hills made of piles of clothing and rocks (they went outside long enough to get the rocks), with branches stuck in them for trees and bits of crumpled-up paper for cannon balls. Carnage raged for an hour as the two armies waged war on each other, each determined to win at all costs. Dead soldiers miraculously came back to life after being felled by cannon balls, and trees and even hills were lowered in the desperate onslaught. Finally the boys declared a truce and went outside, leaving what resembled the aftermath of a natural disaster on the floor of Kip's room.

Kip had a tree house. Arthur was impressed; even his wonderful house did not have a tree house. A secret passage could not compare to a tree house. Kip said his father had built it.

"Is your father a builder?" Arthur asked.

"No," said Kip. "He's the principal at our school."

"Oh," said Arthur. A principal was not very exciting. A builder would have been much more exciting. All principals did was call you into their offices and talk to you about your grades and tell you that your performance needed to improve. Arthur had some experience with this.

"Do you think you will be going to my school?" Kip asked.

"I guess so," Arthur replied. "I suppose Dennis will make me. I don't much like school."

"Me neither," Kip said emphatically. "All except for history. I do like history, because there are lots of battles. I don't like learning the dates, though."

Arthur made a face. "Ugh. Dates are terrible. I don't see why there have to be dates. What are you going to be when you grow up?"

"A pirate," Kip said promptly. "I'm going to be a pirate with a cutlass and a patch over my eye and a wooden leg. What about you?"

"I'm going to be a pilot," Arthur answered. "I was going to be a doctor like Dennis, but he says doctors don't dissect people any more, and that's all the fun. But maybe I'll be a pirate too."

"Yes," Kip said excitedly. "Then we can have a pirate ship, and we can sail around and capture lots of ships and loot, and we'll be so fearsome and terrible, and everyone will be scared of us."

"I know!" Arthur cried. "Let's pretend the tree house is our pirate ship. I'll be Captain Bluenose."

"I'll be Captain Pegleg," Kip said. "And we're fighting a Spanish merchant ship for its doubloons."

As Kip's father walked home from the school where he had been at a meeting, he heard fearsome cries echoing through the neighborhood. At first they were just noises, but as he came nearer to his house he could make out the words.

"I'll slit yer throat, ye scurvy dog!" cried his youngest son's voice in a rough accent.

"And I'll burn yer ships to the ground!" cried another voice, one he did not recognize.

"Avast, or I'll topple yer mainsails!" cried Kip's voice.

"Be gone, or I'll – I'll – cut yer nose off, ye dirty old rat!" threatened the unknown boy. There came a loud *thwack* of wood upon wood, and loud, unrecognizable yells. Mr. Mortimer followed the yells to his backyard, where he found his son and a strange boy engaged in combat with wooden swords up in the tree house. They each wore a crude black patch over one eye, tied on with bits of string, and Kip was wearing one of his father's hats with a chicken feather stuck in it.

Kip caught sight of his father and cried out to his friend, "Avast, there's one of the scurvy Spaniards now." He slithered down the rope ladder, his friend following, and brandished his sword menacingly. They had both tied sticks to their left legs, which Kip's father took to be peg legs.

"Give us all your gold!" Kip shouted.

"I'm afraid I don't have any gold on me," Mr. Mortimer said, emptying his pockets. "Only a bit of toffee. Will that do?"

Kip shrugged. "I suppose so. Hand it over or your life!" He took the toffee and looked it over. He split it in half and gave part to his friend. The boys stopped being pirates for a moment and became boys chewing contentedly on toffee.

"Who is your friend?" Mr. Mortimer asked. "I don't believe we've met."

"Oh, this is Arthur," Kip said. "He lives next door."

"It's very nice to meet you, Arthur." Mr. Mortimer shook Arthur's hand. "So you belong to the family that moved into Mr. Henderson's old house. I've met your brother, Dr. Ramsay."

"Oh," said Arthur. "Nice to meet you too." Kip's father seemed like a very nice person. He was older than Dennis, but not too old, just like Kip's mother. Arthur always felt a little strange about meeting people's mothers and fathers; he was not used to mothers and fathers. Kip's mother and father were not like other mothers and fathers, though. Most mothers and fathers looked at him as if they were very sorry for him. He could not quite understand why. He did not have a mother and a father, but he had Dennis and Lydia, and they were just as good, or bad, depending on how you looked at it and what you were doing. But Kip's mother and father did not look at him as if they were sorry for him, and he did not feel at all strange, the way other people's mothers and fathers made him feel.

"Arthur came over for lunch," Kip explained. "We're playing pirates."

"So I gathered," said Kip's father.

"I'm Captain Pegleg, and Arthur's Captain Bluenose," Kip explained further. "We've been attacking Spanish merchant ships for doubloons."

"I'm sorry I couldn't give you more," Kip's father said. "Well, carry on, Captain Pegleg and Captain Bluenose. Perhaps you'll have better luck soon." He smiled and walked into the house.

"Let's go and see if Miss Rachel has any doubloons," Arthur suggested.

"All right." The boys sheathed their swords and ran off down the sidewalk to Miss Rachel's house. She was on her front porch, sweeping as usual.

"Hand over all your doubloons," Kip cried, unsheathing his sword.

"Or die!" Arthur followed, also unsheathing his sword.

"I see you two have met," Miss Rachel said drily. "I've dreaded that day. We shall have no more peace in this neighborhood, I am sure. Well, come along, I believe I have a few cookies. Will that do?"

The boys looked at each other and grinned. Being pirates was certainly a good trade.

3

Strawberries

Lydia and Mrs. Mortimer met soon, and although Mrs. Mortimer was several years older, they became very good friends. Arthur and Kip were glad because the ladies would often stop by each other's houses for a chat. That kept their attention off of the boys and they could slip away and do whatever they wanted much of the time. It was altogether a very agreeable situation.

Except for one day in August. Mrs. Mortimer and Lydia decided they were going to have a tea party and invite some friends. It was to be held in the Ramsays' house. Lydia had just finished redecorating all of the rooms in the house, so she and Mrs. Mortimer decided it would be a good chance for the ladies of the town to get to know Lydia better and have a sort of house-warming party all at once. That was bad enough, but then Arthur and Kip were pressed into service.

"I want you to pick some strawberries in the back yard after your chores are done," Lydia said to Arthur at breakfast the morning of the tea party. There was a very large bed of strawberries that had been planted years ago by Mr. Henderson, and they had not died, but flourished in great quantities.

Arthur gave a huge sigh and threw his arms out across the table, knocking his glass into Dennis' lap. It only had a little bit of milk left in it, fortunately. "Oh, bother," he groaned. "Why do all those awful old ladies have to come? I don't want to pick strawberries." Arthur liked strawberries, and he often helped himself to the strawberries in the backyard, but he was feeling particularly contrary that day. Perhaps it was the impending threat of the tea party and the fact that he had to dress up in his best clothes and help serve.

"Arthur," said Dennis sternly, "don't argue. Do as Lydia asks, and don't be a problem. If you misbehave, you'll be in big trouble when I get back tonight."

Arthur rolled his eyes. "I'm never bad," he said.

"Arthur," was Dennis' only response.

"Oh, all right, I'll be *good*." Arthur heaved another great sigh. "Can Kip help me?"

"If it's all right with his mother, I don't see why not," Lydia said. "Finish your breakfast and then you can go run over and ask him."

After chores, the boys went out, armed with baskets, to pick strawberries. For a while they picked steadily, although half of what they picked ended up in their mouths. When they had filled one basket, they began to be bored; and rather full of strawberries, they began to feel lazy. Arthur slowly reached into the patch and pulled a strawberry. It was too ripe, and it turned into red mush in his hands. The red juicy pulp on his fingers gave him a feeling of pleasure. Suddenly an impish desire came over him, and quickly he searched for another overripe strawberry. He found one, a nice big one, and let it fly at Kip. *Plop!* It hit him square in the forehead. Juice trickled down his face. Arthur threw back his head and laughed.

He was stopped in the midst of his laugh by a strawberry landing square on his chin. He wiped it away with the back of his hand and cried dramatically, "Oh, I am slain!" He seized another strawberry. For some time strawberries flew hard and fast and battle cries pierced the air. *Plop!* went one on Kip's chest. *Squish!* went one in Arthur's hair. War raged on for a quarter of an hour, then the boys grew tired of it, and remembering that they were supposed to bring in the strawberries, hastily filled up the other basket.

Lydia met them in the hall. She looked cross and tired. "What took you so long," she began, then let out a shriek as she saw the boys' state. Both of them were covered from head to toe in strawberry juice and pulp. Strawberries were tangled in their hair, and Arthur had a red eyelid. They were an awful sight.

Lydia found her tongue at last. "*What* have you been doing?" she exclaimed. "You're both a terrible mess."

Arthur looked down at himself, then at Kip, and burst out laughing. He laughed so hard he could not talk for a full three minutes, so Kip spoke instead. "I'm sorry, Mrs. Ramsay," he said. "We had a strawberry fight."

Lydia sighed and passed her hand over her forehead. "Oh, gracious. Well, run along home, Kip, and take a bath. Arthur! Upstairs, now, and take a bath." She pulled the recumbent figure of Arthur up off the floor and pushed him in the direction of the stairs. Still giggling, Arthur swayed upstairs.

An hour later the preparations for the tea party were all complete. Lydia and Mrs. Mortimer were putting the finishing touches to the splendid array of sandwiches and cakes in the kitchen, and the boys were spotless, dressed in their best clothes. The ladies began to arrive, and Lydia and Mrs. Mortimer stood at the door and greeted them, while Arthur and Kip took their coats and hats and put them in the spare bedroom.

"Well, don't you two look nice," Miss Rachel commented as the boys took her things. "I don't think I've ever seen you so clean before."

When the ladies were all seated in the parlor, Lydia sent the boys into the kitchen to bring out the food. Kip took a plate of sandwiches, and Arthur took a bowl of berries. They passed them to the ladies seated around the parlor, and then placed them on the table in the middle of the room. They brought in the rest of the food after that, and stood by the door in case anyone needed anything. They looked so sweet and clean that the ladies were impressed.

"How sweet your little boys are," said one lady, while Arthur rolled his eyes.

"Is this little Arthur?" asked Mrs. Belmond who lived a few houses down from Miss Rachel.

"It is," Lydia answered. "Say hello to Mrs. Belmond, Arthur."

"'Lo," said Arthur, and gingerly took the hand held out to him. He hated Mrs. Belmond. He had hated her ever since she had called him "Little Arthur."

Lydia, seeing a dangerous light in Arthur's eye, sent him out to get some more berries. The fresh strawberries were a great favorite. Kip went with him to get more sandwiches. On the way to the kitchen, Arthur suddenly had a wild idea. No one knows how he got that idea; there seemed to be a little imp that whispered things to him, and that imp seemed particularly vocal that day. He quickly told his idea to Kip, and they went into the spare bedroom where all the ladies' hats were lying. The hats were fantastic, covered with ribbons and flowers and even a fake bird. Several of the hats had fake fruit on them: strawberries, blueberries, and cherries.

Kip and Arthur took half of the real berries and ate them. They then stripped the hats of their berries and put those in the bowl. Arthur stirred them up, and walked serenely back to the living room.

One lady beckoned to him, and he brought her the bowl of berries. "Delicious berries, Lydia," she said, taking a spoonful and putting them on her plate.

"Thank you," said Lydia, beaming. "The strawberries are fresh from our back yard. Mr. Henderson planted them years ago, and they've done splendidly."

The lady put one of the strawberries in her mouth and ate it. She put another one in her mouth and chewed. And chewed. And chewed some more. After a while she politely spat it out onto her napkin. Other ladies had taken helpings of berries, and one by one they all began to chew and chew. Lydia noticed it, and wondering what was wrong, took a strawberry and tasted it. It was a normal strawberry. She wondered what all the ladies found wrong with them. She was terribly nervous about her first party going wrong. Then she noticed that Arthur and Kip were having convulsions in a corner, and she grew suspicious. She sent Arthur out to get more berries, and after that no one had any problems. Lydia breathed a sigh of relief.

"Come over here, little Arthur," said Mrs. Belmond. Arthur, after a look from Lydia, came. "How old are you, Arthur?" Mrs. Belmond asked.

"Eight," said Arthur stiffly.

"Such a sweet little boy," Mrs. Belmond cooed, reaching out and touching Arthur's cheek.

Arthur swatted her hand away. "Don't touch me," he said crossly. "Your hand stinks."

The ladies gasped. "Arthur George Ramsay," said Lydia, "apologize to Mrs. Belmond."

"Sorry," Arthur muttered, and retreated behind Lydia's chair.

The talk droned on, and the boys began to feel sleepy. Kip was sent out for more cakes, and Arthur was left alone with the boring talk. He was about to fall asleep on his feet when Mrs. Belmond got up to look at some photographs with Lydia. Arthur quickly grabbed a handful of berries, and just as Mrs. Belmond was sitting down, dropped them onto her chair.

Mrs. Belmond uttered a strangled cry and jumped up, clutching her backside. Lydia looked around for Arthur, but he had disappeared. Kip came back with the cakes, and when questioned, said he had not seen his friend. Through the commotion he looked across the room and saw Miss Rachel doubled up in fits of silent laughter.

After that the ladies started to leave. They went into the parlor and discovered their hats. There was instant commotion, and one lady sobbed over her new hat that had been stripped of its artificial berries.

Lydia turned to Kip. "Kip," she said in a voice that sounded like ice, "go and find Arthur and tell him to come here *now*, and no excuses."

Kip ran off and found Arthur outside in one of the bushes which he had hollowed out to make a fort. "Mrs. Ramsay wants you," he said. "She's pretty mad."

Arthur decided he had better not let Lydia wait. Things would just get worse if he did. The boys went back into the house, where they were collared by their respective adults and made to apologize to each of the ladies in turn. They did it with rather ill grace.

Mrs. Belmond was the last to leave. "Laura," Lydia said, "I'm so very sorry for what Arthur did."

"Oh, don't worry about it, my dear," said Mrs. Belmond. "Boys will be boys."

This wise saying did not hold, however, when Dennis came home that evening. He found his wife sewing in the living room, her lips pressed tightly together. Arthur was squirming in a chair beside her. "What's wrong?" Dennis asked, noticing the strained silence.

"Your brother needs to have a talk with you," said Lydia grimly.

"Why? What did he do now?" asked Dennis.

Lydia suddenly became rather hysterical. "What did he do?" she cried. "Oh, where do I even begin? He got into a strawberry fight with Kip and wasted bushels of strawberries ("It wasn't bushels," Arthur interjected, but he was ignored.). He was rude to Mrs. Belmond, and he and Kip pulled all the berries off of the ladies' hats and made them *eat* them, and he put berries on Mrs. Belmond's chair so that she sat on them and ruined her dress, and my party was ruined." Lydia went out abruptly, nearly slamming the door after her.

Arthur heard his full name for the second time that day.

"Arthur George Ramsay, come here," said Dennis.

4

The Prisoner of Nightingale Lane

rthur was alone. As a consequence of their mischief at the tea party, aside from very stern talking-tos, both he and Kip were confined to their respective houses and not allowed to see or talk to each other for three whole days. They weren't even allowed to go outside during that time, which was almost as bad as not being allowed to see each other. It was altogether entirely intolerable, and rather a harsh punishment for so small a misdeed, Arthur thought. He had told Dennis so, but Dennis would not listen to him and instead had subjected him to a long lecture on how good Lydia was to him, and how bad and ungrateful it was for him to do things like that to her, and how he should try to make things easier for her.

Then Dennis said that he and Lydia had wanted to tell him together at a better time, but Lydia had gone to bed, and now was a good time to make Arthur understand why he had to be on his very best behavior. Lydia was having a baby, Dennis said.

"A baby?" Arthur stared at his brother. "A *baby*?"

"Yes, a baby," Dennis said rather shortly. "Lydia needs lots of help, Arthur, and you're making things very hard for her. I'm warning you, if you make any more trouble for her —" he stopped as if he did not know what to say. "The consequences won't be good at all," was all he said finally. "Do you understand?"

"Yes," Arthur said.

"Good," Dennis said and went out. Arthur scratched his head and wondered why everything was suddenly so different now that Lydia was going to have a baby. It was not as if she were dying, after all. It was just a baby. Lots of people had babies.

Lydia was more cheerful the next morning, and she smiled at Arthur when he came down to breakfast. "Good morning, Arthur," she said as if the mischief of the day before had not even happened. "Did you sleep well?"

Arthur nodded and slid into his place at the table. He studied Lydia as she brought the food to the table and called to Dennis that breakfast was ready. She did not look any different, certainly not like she was dying, at any rate.

When Dennis had said grace and they began eating, Lydia looked over at Arthur and smiled. "So Dennis told you we're having a baby," she said. "You're going to be an uncle."

An uncle! Arthur perked up a little. He had not thought that uncles were as young as he was. To him uncles were old, older than Dennis. It would be rather nice to be an uncle, he thought. Not even Dennis was an uncle. He puffed out his chest a little. He felt very important. He wished he could run over and tell Kip the good news, but he could not do so for three whole days.

"Will it be a boy?" he asked.

"We won't know until it's born," Dennis said.

"I hope it's a boy," Arthur said. "I wouldn't want it to be a girl."

"Why not?" Dennis asked, getting up to get more coffee. "I think girls are nice, especially this one." He leaned over and kissed Lydia, and Arthur made a gagging noise and hid his face in his napkin.

"Stop it!" he cried.

"Why?" Dennis asked, and kissed Lydia again. Arthur groaned and kept his face hidden in his napkin while Dennis and Lydia laughed at him.

"Dennis," he asked presently, when all the kissing was over, "why are you so much older than me?"

"Well," Dennis said, "for one, I was born sixteen years before you were."

"I know that," Arthur said. "I mean, *why?*"

Dennis was quiet for a moment, then he said, "Arthur, our mother had three babies between you and me. They were never born, though. They were miscarried."

"Oh," Arthur said. He watched as Lydia reached across the table and squeezed Dennis' hand. He felt rather worried. "Do people always miscarried?" he asked.

"Not too often," Dennis answered. "Our mother had some trouble. She was – well, her body was a little sick, and it was hard for her to have children."

"Oh," Arthur said again, but he still felt a bit worried. Perhaps that was why he was not to cause Lydia any trouble.

"Don't you worry," Lydia said to him. "I'm perfectly healthy, and everything is going splendidly. Right, Dennis?"

"Right," said Dennis, and he looked very happy.

As he was finishing his scrambled eggs and toast, Arthur thought that since Dennis and Lydia were in such a good mood they might release him from his imprisonment. "Could I go see Kip?" he ventured as he was helping Lydia clear the table.

"No, you're still in trouble," Dennis said. "Three days, remember." He kissed Lydia and went to get his hat. "Behave yourself," he called over his shoulder to Arthur.

"I want you to clean your room today," Lydia said.

Arthur opened his mouth to complain, thought better of it, and went up to his room. It was rather a mess. He sat on his bed and surveyed the hills on the floor for several minutes, then picked up a few things and put them away. Exhausted from his efforts, he sat down at his desk to rest. While he was sitting there he spied a notebook in the jumble at his feet. It was a fresh notebook, with nothing written in it. It had been a school notebook, and he was supposed to have written exercises in it, but as he was not fond of writing exercises, he promptly lost it. Unfortunately, his teacher had not taken "I lost my notebook" as an excuse for missing homework, and he had to get another one in which to write his exercises.

An idea hit Arthur suddenly, as ideas often did at odd moments for seemingly no reason at all, at least to everyone but himself. To him there was always a reason, and this idea had been inspired by hearing Dennis talk about a certain writer who was traveling the world. Arthur had always wanted to travel the world; it stood to reason that if he wrote, he had travel the world. Arthur's reasoning always made sense, at least to him. It took a superior intellect to understand these things. He picked up the notebook, found a pencil in the jumble in his desk drawer, chewed it for a full five minutes, and then started to write.

THE PRINS
By Arthur George Ramsay
"Once upon a time ther was a prins. He was a hansom prins, but none of the ladys liked him he was too bad they sed and they were all so kind to his big brother who was not as hansome as our hero.

Our hero was glad none of the lady's liked him, becus he hated ladys, espeshaly little girls becus people always said the little girls were so sweet and pretty but our hero hated them. Im never going to get married he said im going to become a hermit. You cant do that sed his father. Yes I can sed our hero. No you cant becus you have to becum a brave nite and rescyou lady's fare said his father. Well ill become a nite but I wont rescyou lady's fare said our hero. So he becam a nite and he did many brav thins. He was the bravist nite in the hol world. Wenever somwun wanted his batls fot he asked the prins to fite them for him becus the prins always wun wen he fot batls. He was teribly strong and brav and he cood kil ten bad men with wun blow. He becam very famus. One day a king said he had to rescyou his doter who was capterd by a dragun. So are hero set out becus the king said he wood chop of his hed if he didnt. He fownd the dragon and he sed Im supposed to rescyou a lady fare but I hate prinseses, so Im not. I like you sed the dragon come and live with me. So our hero came and lived with the dragon, and they ate prinseses for ther supper and little girls for ther brekfast. For lunch they had left over females. The dragon and the prins lived happily ever after and soon ther wer no more females left in the land."

THE END

Arthur leaned back and surveyed his work with great satisfaction. What a good story it was. And what a good author he was. It was much, much better than those awful fairy tales where the prince rescued the princess, and they lived happily ever after and kissed each other and all that disgusting stuff. He sighed contentedly and signed his name at the bottom of the paper with a flourish. Someday, when he was a great and renowned author, he would sign his books like that. Arthur George Ramsay, G.A.I.T.W.; W.T. (That stood for Greatest Author in the World, World Traveler.) How good that sounded! Then they would all see. Oh yes, they would see. Then they would not make him clean up his room, and other odious things like that.

Arthur thought for a bit, then decided that he would try his hand at some poetry. He was not terribly crazy about poetry; it was rather silly, he thought. There was some good poetry, the stuff about knights and kings and all that, but on the whole it was silly. But this world-traveling writer Dennis had talked about wrote poetry as well as books, and if he wanted to travel the world, Arthur would have to write poetry as well. His poetry would be much better than the average, of course. He chewed his pencil for a long moment, then started to write.

THE KING
By Arthur George Ramsay

Wuns there was a king
He was a very grate king
And he cood sing
Much lowder than anething
He had a great big sord
and he fot with it wen he was bord
He had a grate big sheeld

That wood make peeple yeeld
He had a great big speer
That wood make peeple feer
He had a grate big hors
To rid on of corse
He had a grate big mase
To nok peeple into spase
He had a great big casl —

Here Arthur stopped because he could not think of a rhyme for "castle". He ran over some words in his head, but could not find the right one. Bassle, dassle, fassle, gassle — no, none of them worked. He had never even heard of such words. He scribbled out the last line and wrote:

He had a great big army

But that line did not work either because he couldn't think of a rhyme for army. Barmy, carmy, darmy, farmy — none of those words worked either. Arthur decided that was a good place to end his poem, especially since he heard Lydia coming up the stairs. She would come in to make sure he was cleaning, and if he was not cleaning, she would be angry. Arthur shoved the notebook into the top drawer of his desk and bent down to pick up a shirt lying at his feet.

"Are you working?" Lydia asked, poking her head in the door.

"Mmmhmm," Arthur said.

Lydia surveyed the room with a skeptical eye. "You've been in here for half an hour, and I don't see a dent in the mountains on the floor. You'd better be done in half an hour or you won't get any dessert."

Arthur sighed. "All right, all right. I don't know why I have to clean up anyway. I like it messy."

Lydia gave him a look and went out, saying, "Half an hour."

Arthur sighed again and began to pick up his things. His family was so cruel to him. First he could not see Kip for three whole days, or go outside, and now Lydia was making him clean up his room. It just was not fair. They treated him like a prisoner. That was what he was, a poor prisoner abandoned in a dark and dismal cell without food or water. He began to heave deep, abysmal sighs as he cleaned his room, and several times he moaned in agony. Once Lydia poked her head in the door and asked why he was making noises like a sick cow.

"I am not making noises like a sick cow," Arthur said with dignity. "I'm a prisoner."

"Oh," said Lydia. "How terrible." With those very unsympathetic words she went away, leaving the poor prisoner to his fate.

Arthur picked up a few more things and put them away, then stuffed the rest into his closet. When he had finished he sat down at his desk again and took out his notebook. He thought for a while, then began once more to write.

THE PRISNER
By Arthur George Ramsay

In a deep dark prisin under the casle was a prisiner. This prisner's name was Archibald. Archibald wasnt very old. He wasnt very yung eether. He was a yung man hoo had been throne in the prisin by his wikid stepfamily hoo hated him he was a very smart yung man and his stepfamily was very stupid and they hated smart peeple so they throow all the smart peeple into ther prisin. Archibald had a frend hoos name was Cristofer Cristofer was very smart too so the stepfamily throow him into the prisin to. Archilbald coodnt talk to Cristofer becus Cristofer was on the other side of the casle in a prisin cel. Wun day Archibald sed to himself --- it all

(Arthur almost wrote the actual word, but decided against it. He would probably get in trouble for writing swear words, even though grownups did it all the time.)

I dont want to liv in a prisin cel for the rest of my lif I need to get out. He lookd arownd him but all he cood see was the cold gray stons of the prisin cel Ther wasnt even a window. So Archibald wated and wated and thot and thot and wun day a man cam to see him this man was wun of the jalers. Let me out, --- you, Archibald sed. Never sed the jaler. Your stepfather sed you had to stay in here until you rot. Well I wont Archibald sed ill get out. The jaler lafed nastily no you wont he sed. Youll never get out. Well see about that Archibald sed and he punched the jaler hard in the nose The jaler fell over and Archibald took his dager. Ha ha Archibald lafed now

41

weell see whos rite. He climed over the body of the jaler and hurryed out of the prisin cell. He went and fownd his frend Cristofer Cristofer was very sick but Archibald caried him out of the prisin on his bake he was very strong. Then a grate cry went out all over the casle becus they had fond out that Archibald and Cristofer had escapde his stepfather came out with a bunch of nites with sords, but Archibald fot them all of. He grabed a hors and throwing Cristofer on the back of the hors he rode of into the nite. Then he met a wich and asked her to put a curs on his stepfamily and gave her many gold coins in return. The wich put a spel on his stepfamily and they all turnd into pigs and Archibald and Cristofer went back to the casle and becam kings and they used the pigs that usd to be his stepfamily to eat all the weeds in the garden Archibald and Cristofer became the gratest kings in the hole world even grater than king Arthur. King Arthur was the king of kings but they wer the kings of kings of kings.
THE END

Arthur finished just as Lydia came in, carrying a pile of laundry. "Are you done?" she asked, looking around skeptically.

"Of course," Arthur said in an offended tone.

"Hmm," was all Lydia said and moved toward the closet to put the clothes away.

"Oh, Lydia," Arthur said, trying to divert her attention from the closet, "I have something to tell you."

"Hmm?" Lydia's hand was on the closet door.

"I mean, I have something I need to show you," Arthur said hastily.

"In a minute," Lydia said.

"It's very urgent," Arthur said. "I need you to see it right now."

Lydia turned away from the closet. "What is it?"

Arthur franticly racked his brain, and just as he was about to give up hope he remembered a scratch he had gotten a few days before. "Here," he said, "I cut myself. I'm going to bleed to death."

"Let me see," Lydia said. She put the pile of laundry on the bed and went to stand in front of Arthur.

"Oh, I don't know if you can do anything about it," Arthur said. "It's really bad. Dennis might have to amputate it."

"Don't be silly," Lydia said. "If it were that bad, you would be screaming all over the house. Let me see it."

Arthur showed her his scratch.

"Why, that's just a little scratch," Lydia said. "You're certainly not going to bleed to death. Just put a bandage on it." She picked up the pile of clothes and moved towards the closet again.

Arthur was getting desperate. "Lydia, your bread's burning!" he cried out.

Lydia gave him a funny look. "I'm not baking bread," she said. "What is the matter with you, Arthur?" She turned the door handle and gave a little yelp as a pile of clothes and books tumbled out. "Arthur Ramsay!" she cried. "You certainly did not clean up your room!"

"Yes, I did," Arthur said. "It's clean, isn't it?"

Lydia looked decidedly cross. "No dessert for you. Now clean it all up. I'm going to come back and check in fifteen minutes."

Arthur grumbled under his breath as Lydia went out. It looked like it was time to find a witch. He could use a few pigs.

5

Arthur and Kip Go to School

All too soon the summer was over, and one evening at dinner Lydia said, "School starts the day after tomorrow, Arthur. I've talked to Mr. Mortimer, and he said you are to be in Kip's class."

A deep sense of dark, impending doom filled Arthur's soul. He threw out his arms in dismay and knocked over his glass. "What!" he cried. "School! I can't go to school!"

"Why not?" Dennis asked.

Arthur groped for an answer. "I just can't. I'm – I'm allergic to school."

"From past experience I know you have a certain aversion to school, but you're certainly not allergic to it," Dennis said. "Don't argue; you're going."

"Tomorrow we can go out and get you some new notebooks and things," Lydia said. "We should get you a

45

new pair of shoes, too. Your old school shoes are probably too small by now."

That was no comfort at all. Arthur didn't care about new shoes, and notebooks and pencils meant lessons. It was a depressing thought, and altogether a depressing future that presented itself. All the next day Arthur did all he could to get sick, as he did every year before school started. If he got sick, perhaps he would not have to go to school. He sat in puddles. He ate an old, wormy apple. He put his face up close to Kip's little brother who had a cold, and even went so far as to let Jamie sneeze all over him. He went to bed on Sunday night hoping that he would wake up with a fever or even a cold, but Monday morning came and he had never felt better. There was not even the slightest hint of a sniffle.

He dressed slowly. Lydia had to call him twice to come down to breakfast. Arthur put on his most melancholy face and dragged his feet as he went downstairs.

"Good morning," Lydia said. "Did you sleep well?"

"Terribly," Arthur moaned. "I think I'm sick. I feel terrible. I think I have a fever. I think I'm going to die."

Dennis felt Arthur's forehead. "Nonsense," he said. "You're just pretending, and you are certainly not going to die. As far as I know, school has never killed anyone. Hurry up and eat, or you'll be late for school. No, you may not be late."

"Kip's mother phoned and said Kip would walk with you to school," Lydia said. "I have your lunch ready for you. Hurry up, Arthur. You're as slow as molasses this morning."

After breakfast Lydia nearly pushed Arthur out the door, and he went to meet Kip. Kip was very clean, and he had new shoes, too. He looked just as gloomy as Arthur felt.

"I didn't get sick," Arthur said sadly.

"Me either," Kip said. "And I tried so hard." And they both sighed lugubriously.

They started off to school together, waving to Miss Rachel as they walked by her house.

"Off to school?" Miss Rachel asked.

"Yes," they both said gloomily.

"I remember a time when I hated going to school," Miss Rachel said. "Then my mother told me that I would have to go to school for a very long time, and there was no way out of it, so I might as well enjoy it."

"What did you do?" Kip asked.

"I enjoyed it," Miss Rachel replied. "You can enjoy anything if you've a mind to. Now off with you, or you'll be late."

Arthur and Kip looked doubtful. Usually Miss Rachel said smart things, but this time her sage advice seemed a little less than that. There were certain things that could never be enjoyed, such as taking medicine, or cleaning one's room. Arthur and Kip waved goodbye to Miss Rachel and continued their way, talking about anything but school. It was not a popular subject with them. They considered skipping school and playing pirates somewhere, but Kip decided that since his father was the principal it would not be a very good idea. He had very uncomfortable memories of a time two years ago when he had skipped school, and his father had promised certain very dire consequences if it ever happened again.

They arrived at school just in time for the first bell. Arthur had to go see Mr. Mortimer first. Mr. Mortimer seemed very different sitting behind the big principal's desk. He was a lot scarier there than he normally was. Normally he was a very nice man who was Kip's father, but here behind the big, shiny desk he was one of the people that Arthur did not get along with very well, one of those people who sent Dennis pieces of paper with Arthur's grades on them, and made Dennis say he was disappointed in Arthur.

Everything went well, however, and soon Mr. Mortimer dismissed the boys and they went to their classroom. Arthur recognized Angel Lidden and one or two of the boys from church, but most of the children were boys and girls he did not know. He and Kip found desks close to the back of the room, conveniently near a window out of which they could look when they were bored, and sat down to wait for the teacher.

Their teacher was a little old lady named Miss Brentwood. She was a small and very mousy sort of lady. Everything about her reminded the boys of a mouse. Even her hair was gray like a mouse's, and she had a funny habit of wrinkling her nose as if she were smelling cheese.

The day started off very badly. As soon as Miss Brentwood entered the room, Arthur and Kip took a great dislike to her. Their dislike became even greater when Miss Brentwood said in a cheery voice, "Good morning, boys and girls. I am Miss Brentwood." She spelled it out on the board for them: B-r-e-n-t-w-o-o-d. She led the class in a prayer, a very sappy one about Jesus leading the sweet little children. "Let's all stand up and sing a song to start the day off *just* right, shall we? Does anyone know of a good morning sort of song?"

One of the girls raised her hand, and Miss Brentwood called her up to the front of the room. She had the girl sing the song to them once, and then they all had to stand up and sing along:

Good morning, good morning,
Good morning to you!
"Good morning!" the birds call,
They call out to you.

All birdies and beasties
Are up and away;
"Good morning," they're calling –
"We'll have a nice day!"

Arthur and Kip stood up with the rest of their class. The song was the most horrid, sappy song they could imagine. They sang it, but they sang it just as they thought it should be sung. The result was that at times Miss Brentwood could hear low growls, at other times high shrieks, and in between all sorts of strange sounds. When the song was over she asked, "Who was singing in that very unpleasant way?"

"A bird," Arthur said sweetly, and he and Kip burst into giggles.

Miss Brentwood frowned. "Arthur and Christopher-Paul," she said, "do not do that in the future. We must all blend our voices together like one happy family. Isn't that right, children?"

Arthur rolled his eyes as far as they would go and lolled back in his seat. He looked around him and paid no attention to the lesson, which happened to be math. He had never liked math. He had never liked most subjects, but math and he were particular enemies. He looked instead at the girl sitting in front of him. She had long black braids hanging down her back and she was wearing a frilly pink dress. Arthur did not like either frills or pink. He was about to pin one of her braids to the back of her chair, but he was foiled.

"Laura Roberts, will you demonstrate this problem for us?" asked Miss Brentwood. She of the black braids stood up and made her way to the blackboard where she began to demonstrate the problem in a neat, clear hand. Miss

Brentwood praised her for her excellent work, and Laura beamed.

Laura sat down and Miss Brentwood called Arthur up to demonstrate the next problem. With leaden feet Arthur slowly made his way up to the blackboard. He stood with his hand poised, ready for the help which did not come.

"Well, Arthur, aren't you going to begin?" came Miss Brentwood's voice behind him.

"Um," said Arthur.

"Well?"

"Um," said Arthur again.

"I don't believe you know the lesson," said Miss Brentwood. "Well, you may sit down, and pay more attention from now on."

Arthur spent all of the next lesson carefully pinning Laura Roberts' long braids to the back of her chair so that when she stood up she cried out in pain. Miss Brentwood was very cross with Arthur, though she tried not to show it, and she made him stay in during recess and wipe off all the blackboards. That was not too bad, since the blackboard erasers made such lovely clouds of dust. That is, as long as Miss Brentwood was not looking.

After recess, Arthur and Kip, bored nearly to death, made faces at the other children when Miss Brentwood's back was turned. They were such gruesome faces that all the children laughed. Miss Brentwood discovered who the culprits were right away, for they were the only ones not laughing, and made them write out "I will not make faces in school" one hundred times.

Next, when Arthur was called up to the board again, he managed to spill Miss Brentwood's glass of water all over her desk. One of the boys laughed at him and made a face, and Arthur picked up the glass and hurled it at the boy. It narrowly missed him and sailed out of the open window, landing on the head of a lady who happened to be passing by at the moment. Miss Brentwood told Arthur to stand up by the blackboard with his back towards the class. He took a piece of chalk from the ledge, and when the teacher was not looking, scrawled hideous faces on the blackboard which he titled, "Miss Brentwood." Miss Brentwood caught him, gave his hand a few light taps with the ruler, and sent him to another corner away from the blackboard. There Arthur whistled under his breath until Miss Brentwood in exasperation sent him to the principal's office. Mr. Mortimer talked to him sternly about how he must behave, and sent him back to apologize to Miss Brentwood.

Poor Miss Brentwood was already worn to a frazzle and at her wit's end, and an apology did not help much. When Arthur and Kip started throwing spitballs and the other boys joined in, she cut the day short. The children ran out with delighted cries, but Miss Brentwood collapsed into her chair and wondered what in the world had convinced her to be a teacher instead of a secretary.

Arthur and Kip walked home feeling very contented with themselves and the world at large. They did not think of the impending doom that was sure to come when they went home, though Kip had a little bit of a nagging uncomfortableness in the back of his mind. The afternoon was bright and clear and still warm, and they were out of school early. Adventures called to them, and they jumped to answer the call. They walked down to the end of the street, by unspoken consent avoiding their houses, and turned the corner into the Lot. The Lot was an overgrown piece of land that apparently did not belong to anyone, so the children of the town had taken it over as their playground. It was a wonderful place to play, and now Arthur and Kip had it all to themselves.

They were soon lost in an exciting game of pirates, with the old, creaky playground set serving as a pirate ship. They forgot about school and about authorities who no doubt waited with eloquent words to convince them of their wrongdoing. The only thing that mattered now was that the scurvy dog Captain Bucktooth was trying to get their gold. His ship had drawn up close to theirs after much firing of cannons, and now his yelling hoard of dirty pirates were trying to board. Yelling and brandishing their swords, Captain Bluenose and Captain Pegleg fought valiantly to protect their ship, but they were soon outnumbered, and the enemy pressed closer. Captain Bluenose fell from the stroke of an enemy sword with a loud and dramatic cry. "Help me; I'm dying!" he called to his comrade.

Captain Pegleg immediately pulled a vial of magic potion out of his pocket and tossed it to Captain Bluenose. Captain Bluenose drained the vial, and was immediately restored to health and life, with twice the vigor and strength he had previously possessed. "Aye, now we'll make them run!" Captain Bluenose bellowed, jumping to his feet.

"Aye, aye, that we will!" replied his comrade, also in a healthy bellow.

Gradually, the enemy was beaten back and locked in chains below decks until such a time as they should walk the plank. Once the two captains had counted their loot they made all of the enemy pirates walk the plank. The enemy neatly deposited in the ocean, the captains set out to bury their loot, and civil war ensued because they could not decide where they should bury it. A physical struggle began, along with several choice words.

"I said *there!*" panted Captain Pegleg.

"Well, I said over by the tree!" panted Captain Bluenose.

"I don't have to do what you tell me!" cried the recumbent figure of Captain Pegleg.

"Yes you do!" howled Captain Bluenose. "I'm two days older than you!"

"Well, I've lived here longer!"

Failing to find an appropriate retort to this claim, Captain Bluenose spluttered, "You – you platypus!"

Captain Pegleg instantly threw back an insult of his own. "You smelly old hog!"

"You hemophiliac!" Captain Bluenose had a store of good medical words from listening to his brother.

"You – you – oomph!" Captain Pegleg had meant to utter something else, but having the breath knocked out of him, that was all that came out. He caught his breath and charged at his opponent.

They rolled and tumbled around again until they realized that dusk was falling, and their grumbling stomachs told them that it must be nearly time for dinner. Their animosity gone, they strolled home, talking about different pirate ships they had read about. They had completely forgotten about the events of the day, and their consciences were untroubled.

They parted in front of Arthur's house. Kip said farewell to his friend and went on to his house. His family, all except for his father, was sitting down to dinner. "There you are," his mother said. "I was just going to send Jerry to find you. Daddy's going to be home soon. He had to stay late. Hurry and wash up."

Then it hit him. Kip remembered what had happened earlier that day, and he felt distinctly uncomfortable. The last time he had skipped school was too fresh in his memory, and he had a feeling that his father's lateness had something to do with him. He washed his hands and sat down to eat a plate of chicken pot pie. It was very good, and was also his favorite, and he was finishing his second helping when his father came home.

Mr. Mortimer looked very tired. Mrs. Mortimer kissed him and dished up some pie for him. "How was the first day?" she asked.

Mr. Mortimer made a blustery sound, and said, "I need to eat first. And then –" turning a stern eye on his youngest – "I need to have a talk with you, Christopher-Paul."

Kip shrank down in his chair. The use of his full name never boded well.

"Well, what happened?" Mrs. Mortimer asked after her husband had finished his first helping of chicken pot pie and was working on his second.

Mr. Mortimer looked like a kettle that was going to boil over. "It seems," he said, "that Kip and Arthur were so bad in class today that Miss Brentwood has had a nervous breakdown and quit."

There was a very long silence, and Kip shrank farther down into his chair with all of his family's eyes fixed on him. His father swallowed his last forkful of chicken pot pie and stood up. "Christopher-Paul," he said, "come with me." Kip got up, feeling as if he were going to the executioner's block, and followed his father out of the room.

Next door, Arthur was undergoing a similar fate to his friend. He had vaguely hoped that Dennis would not hear about his escapades at school, but Mr. Mortimer had telephoned Dennis before dinner, and Dennis had plenty to say about the misdeeds of the day. Perhaps, then, Arthur's fate was worse than Kip's, for he got his punishment on an empty stomach.

6

Arthur and Kip Go to School Again

There was no school for the third grade the next day since there was no teacher and Mr. Mortimer was unable to find a substitute at such short notice. Arthur and Kip were excited when they found out, but their excitement was short-lived, for they had to stay in their respective houses and do lessons under the watchful eyes of Mrs. Mortimer and Lydia. It was a painful time for all involved.

So it was that everyone except for Arthur and Kip was very happy when a new teacher was found. Mr. Mortimer came home one evening and announced that he had found a replacement teacher, a young man by the name of Mr. Reid, who was willing to start right away. "He's very competent," Mr. Mortimer said. "He has been at a boys' boarding school up until now. They won't be giving this one a nervous breakdown." And he fixed Kip with a stern eye. Mrs. Mortimer went to telephone Lydia, who was very happy to hear the news. She did not very much like having to teach Arthur.

"I wish they hadn't found a new teacher," Arthur grumbled.

"You be quiet," said Dennis. "It's because of you that everyone has gone through so much trouble."

"Well, they didn't have to," Arthur said.

He received a look identical to the one Kip had received from his father. "If you cause any more trouble, I swear I'll send you to boarding school," Dennis said. He was very angry about what Arthur had done, and he had already carried out his threat about something bad happening if Arthur made trouble for Lydia. Arthur did not think Dennis would actually send him to boarding school, but all the same he was very wary and tried his best to be helpful to Lydia from then on.

The next day at school, everyone was curious to see the new teacher. He was not much older than Dennis, Arthur thought. He was tall and thin and had a shock of red hair like Kip's, only Mr. Reid's hair was not curly and had a tendency to stand on end. To Arthur and Kip, he did not really look like a teacher. In their experience teachers were older and rather nervous-looking, and generally female. Neither of them had ever actually had a male teacher.

The new teacher introduced himself as Mr. Reid, and he did not write his name on the board, because, he said, it was a simple enough name to remember. He led the class in a prayer that sounded grand, all about the Holy Spirit lighting fires in people's hearts. "Now," he said, "please open your poetry books to page twenty-one. Yes?" he said to Angel Lidden, who raised her hand.

"Aren't we going to sing?" asked Angel.

"Sing?" Mr. Reid looked puzzled.

"Yes," said Angel. "Miss Brentwood had us sing a song at the beginning of school. To start the day out just right, you know."

"Sing?" Mr. Reid repeated. "Good heavens, no. You would not want to hear me sing anyway. We're going to learn a poem. It's from *The Wind in the Willows*, by Kenneth Grahame. Have any of you read it? Good. I used to love this poem when I was your age. I'll read it to you first, and then we'll start memorizing the first few lines." Mr. Reid did not look at the book, though, as he recited,

The world has held great Heroes,
As history-books have showed;
But never a name to go down to fame
Compared with that of Toad.

The clever men at Oxford
Know all that there is to be knowed.
But they none of them know one half as much

60

As intelligent Mr. Toad!

The animals sat in the Ark and cried,
Their tears in torrents flowed.
Who was it said, "There's land ahead?"
Encouraging Mr. Toad!

The Army all saluted
As they marched along the road.
Was it the King? Or Kitchener?
No. It was Mr. Toad!

The Queen and her Ladies-in-waiting
Sat at the window and sewed.
She cried, "Look! who's that handsome man?"
They answered, "Mr. Toad."

"That's such a silly poem," Angel Lidden said when Mr. Reid had finished. "It doesn't make any sense. And you shouldn't say 'knowed.'"

"It's a story, Angel," Mr. Reid said. "It's not necessarily supposed to make sense. And if you're a good writer, you can sometimes break the rules."

Angel turned her nose up. "Well, I don't like it."

Arthur was cheered. He liked *The Wind in the Willows* very much. It was one of his favorite books. And if Angel Lidden did not like the poem, that made it all the better.

After they had memorized the first stanza of the poem, they turned to math. Arthur did not pay attention. He scrawled on a piece of paper, oblivious to the fact that Mr. Reid had his eye on him.

"Arthur Ramsay," Mr. Reid said at last. When Arthur looked up Mr. Reid told him to come up and demonstrate the next problem. "No excuses," he said. "Come up right now." He must have been told of the escapades of the first day.

Arthur ambled up to the blackboard, picked up the chalk, and studied the blackboard. Mr. Reid waited in silence for some time, and when Arthur made no sign of demonstration, he calmly told him to sit down and study the lesson again. Arthur did not study it, of course. He spent the rest of the class drawing pictures all over his math book, most of which involved math and schools being destroyed in various ways.

Science was after recess. For science, Mr. Reid said, they were all going down to the river to catch tadpoles. They would study the tadpoles over the next few weeks. The children were very excited. None of their teachers had ever done anything like this before. Ten minutes later they were tramping off to the river, Mr. Reid at their head. While they were catching tadpoles, Arthur knocked Harry Price, a boy whom he did not particularly like, into the river. After Harry, "blubbering like a baby," as Arthur said, was fished out, Mr. Reid pulled Arthur aside and asked him why he had done it.

"It was an accident," Arthur said innocently.

"That's not true," said Mr. Reid.

"You think I'm lying?" Arthur asked in an injured tone.

"No, I think you're telling a fib."

Arthur scowled.

"Now go apologize to Harry," Mr. Reid commanded.

"Wh-a-t?" Arthur was incredulous.

"You heard me. Go apologize to Harry."

Arthur sighed and made a rather grudging apology to Harry, who looked smug despite his bedraggled state.

When they had caught enough tadpoles in a jam jar, they went back to school, where they placed the tadpoles in a fishbowl. They learned about tadpoles, and school was over for the day.

As they were all getting up to go home, Mr. Reid said, "Arthur, please stay; I want to talk to you." Arthur sighed and sat down again. When all the children were gone, Mr. Reid beckoned to Arthur, and he came up and stood in front of the big desk. Arthur sighed again. He knew what was coming. His teachers were always lecturing him on good behavior in school. Therefore, he was very surprised when Mr. Reid leaned back in his chair, arms behind his head, and just looked at him. Arthur began to feel rather uncomfortable.

At last Mr. Reid spoke. "Arthur, how much do you actually learn at school?"

Arthur stared at him.

"Well?" Mr. Reid prompted.

"I learn lots," Arthur said.

"Such as how to do multiplication?" Arthur had the distinct feeling that his teacher was laughing at him, though he was not actually laughing out loud. "Now look here, Arthur," Mr. Reid went on. "Your brother is a very good doctor. Kip's father is a very good principal. I'm here teaching you hoodilums. How do you suppose we got those jobs?"

Arthur shrugged.

"Because we all went to college. And the only reason we went to college is because we did our lessons when we were young."

"Did you?" Arthur asked curiously.

Mr. Reid coughed. "We won't go into that right now. Arthur, what do you want to be when you grow up?"

"A pirate," Arthur said.

Mr. Reid made a funny sort of sound that was almost a laugh, but not quite. "A very fine profession, I'm sure," he said. "But don't you think that pirates need to learn things?"

Arthur considered this. "No," he said after reflection. "I don't think so."

"But pirates have to know how to sail ships, and read maps, and count their gold and all that, don't they?" Mr. Reid asked.

"I suppose so," said Arthur.

"Then they have to go to school."

Arthur sighed. "I suppose I should be a pilot then."

"Pilots have to go to school too."

Arthur sighed again. "So I guess I have to go to school anyway."

Mr. Reid nodded. "That's right."

"What are you going to do if I don't do my lessons?" Arthur challenged.

"What am I going to do?" Mr. Reid leaned forward and pointed at Arthur with his pencil. "*I* am not going to do anything, but *you* are going to stay in after school and learn everything you did not learn in class. If you prefer to take a break during school hours, very well, but you will have to make up for it afterwards. Take your math book and start at page ten."

Arthur sat down and began to read about multiplication. It took him a long time to finish his lessons, and by the time he was done, dusk was falling. Mr. Reid said, "I'll walk you to your street." They walked through the dusky streets together and Mr. Reid told Arthur about a book he had read when he was not much older than Arthur. It was about pirates. "Do you know," he said, "I wanted to be a pirate once, when I was young."

"Why didn't you?" Arthur asked. They had reached the end of Nightingale Lane.

"I grew up," Mr. Reid said, "and realized that there were much more important things to be done in the world."

"Being grown-up must be so boring," Arthur said.

Mr. Reid smiled. "Oh, I don't know about that. I can't say being a teacher has been particularly boring, especially when I have students like you."

"Well, I'd still rather not grow up," Arthur said.

Mr. Reid smiled again. "Don't we all wish that. Well, I'll be seeing you in the morning. Good night, Arthur."

"Good night," Arthur said. He skipped home. Perhaps school was not so bad after all.

7

The Maestro

One night in the bleak days of November, Dennis came home to dinner with news. "There's a concert tomorrow night," he said.

"What's a concert?" Arthur asked around a mouthful of potato.

"You know, musicians playing music for an audience," Dennis said. "Don't talk with your mouth full."

"Oh," said Arthur. That did not sound very exciting. He went on eating his dinner. He was of the age when boys would rather be doing something, and had not as yet discovered the joys of sitting quietly and listening to a piece of music. Besides, he had too many bad memories of school concerts, which were never shining moments for him.

"Anyway," Dennis went on, more to Lydia than to the disinterested Arthur, "a violinist is playing with the orchestra at the concert hall in town. I thought you'd like it, so I bought three tickets."

Lydia got up and went around the table to kiss Dennis. She looked very happy. Lydia loved music, and she especially loved violin music. Her older brother, whose name was Peter Benson, was a violinist. Arthur had never met him because he lived in a place called Vienna that was somewhere far away. Arthur was not very good at geography.

"Do I have to go?" Arthur asked.

"Yes, you do," Dennis said. "We're not going to leave you here alone."

"Can't I stay with the Mortimers?"

"The Mortimers are going, too."

Arthur was relieved. If Kip was going, then it could not be too bad. He and Kip discussed the upcoming concert in the tree house that night. Kip was also a bit dubious about it. He had not been to many concerts before, but he had not liked the few he had been to, though he liked music. "It's just so long," he said. "You have to sit for so long." Arthur agreed that this was indeed a problem. Sitting for a long period of time put a toll on a boy.

The next day, Saturday, they had dinner early, and Lydia made Arthur take a bath. After his bath he had to put on his best suit that was reserved for special occasions such as Christmas and Easter. He hoped he didn't have to wear a tie. It was bad enough to take a bath and wear a suit. But Lydia took out his tie, and he complained so much that

Dennis had to come and tell him to behave. Arthur groaned as Dennis was tying his tie. "Are you trying to strangle me?" he complained.

"Don't be ridiculous," was Dennis' response.

"Pirates don't wear ties," Arthur grumbled.

"When you are grown up and have your own pirate ship, you can decide whether you want to wear ties or not," Dennis said. "Stand still, or I just might strangle you."

Arthur had never been to the concert hall before, and he was rather impressed. It was so big, and there was so much red velvet and gold. They were a little early, so they waited in the lobby until the Mortimers came. They went in and found good seats, and Arthur and Kip requested permission to sit together.

"If you sit still and don't make a sound," Mrs. Mortimer said. This was better than nothing, and the boys were seated together on the right side of Mr. Mortimer and to the left of Lydia. Arthur looked at the program the man at the door had given him. It said the first piece was something with a name in a foreign language by someone named Beethoven.

"Don't you want to know what it is?" he heard Dennis ask Lydia in a teasing voice.

"Stop it!" Lydia said, and hit him lightly. Lydia said she never looked at programs beforehand. She liked to be surprised. Arthur had asked her what if it was something she did not like and she said she liked most music, so it was all right.

The lights in the audience went off, and then there was a lot of clapping as a man wearing a black coat with tails came onto the stage. He was carrying a thin white stick. Arthur wondered what he would do with the stick. Perhaps he played a drum. But no, there was already someone sitting behind the big drums, and the man with the stick was going up to the big black stand in front of the orchestra and bowing.

"Who's that man?" Arthur whispered to Lydia.

"He's the conductor," Lydia whispered back.

"Like on a train?"

"No."

"What's the stick for?" Arthur began again.

"Shh," Lydia whispered. "You'll see."

Arthur did not really see. The conductor lifted up the stick and began to wave it around, and all the people on stage began to play their instruments. Arthur wondered if it was a magic stick.

The first piece of music on the program was not terribly interesting, and the drummer did not once pick up his drumsticks. Arthur nearly fell asleep. He was jerked to consciousness by the sound of people clapping. The music had come to an end. He whispered to Lydia, "Is there more?"

"Shh," said Lydia. "Yes, there is." She was looking very happy, like she did when she played the record player at home, but even more so.

The conductor left the stage, and in a moment came back with a man who was carrying a violin. Lydia gasped and straightened up in her seat. Arthur looked over at her, and she looked even happier, and reached out to grasp Dennis' hand. She must really like the violin a lot, Arthur thought.

The conductor started waving his stick around again, and the orchestra started playing again. The violinist stood silently in front of the orchestra at first, and then he suddenly started playing. The music grabbed at Arthur, and the violin player swaying back and forth on the stage suddenly became the most amazing thing in the world. The drums banged away, but Arthur paid attention only to the violin. Lydia played violin music all the time on the record player, but this was so real, and so different. Arthur sat still, his eyes fixed on the man with the violin, and did not move once. The violinist played and played. He played three different pieces of music, one sort of fast, one slow and very sad sounding, and another fast one. Arthur did not want him to stop, but he did, and Arthur was jerked out of his enthralled state by applause. All around him people were standing up and cheering, and Lydia was crying with her arms around Dennis.

Arthur hardly heard the next piece after the violinist left the stage. He was still lost in the sheer wonder of the violin music. It was not just the music itself – it was the violin, which to him seemed to be beauty itself, although he did not and could not quite express it that way. It was wonderful, and very much alive, that much he knew.

The lights came on, and people started to leave. Arthur followed Dennis and Lydia out into the lobby, where they stood until the crowd began to thin. Miss Rachel came up to them and talked to Lydia and Dennis for a while. Then she turned to Arthur and said, "So, Tot Feet, how did you like the concert?"

"It was great!" Arthur said enthusiastically.

"Well, I'm glad you have some taste," Miss Rachel said. She said goodbye and walked away.

The Mortimers came out of the hall. Mrs. Mortimer gave Lydia a hug and said, "Dennis told us. I'm so happy for you." They talked for a bit, and Arthur and Kip wandered around the lobby until the Mortimers left.

"Are we going to go?" Arthur asked.

"Not yet," Dennis said. "We're going to see someone."

Arthur did not really want to stay, but he felt better about it when Dennis had talked to an attendant, and they went backstage. Perhaps he would get to see the violins. When they were backstage they went to one of the dressing rooms and Dennis knocked on the door. It was opened by the violin player. Lydia cried, "Peter!" and ran into his arms. They hugged each other for a long time, and Lydia started crying again. Finally they let go of each other, and the violin player shook Dennis' hand.

Lydia put her hand on Arthur's shoulder. "Arthur," she said, "this is my brother, Peter."

Arthur stared in amazement. "You mean the one who plays the violin?" he asked.

"The same," Lydia's brother Peter said. He shook Arthur's hand. "I'm glad to meet you. Lydia has written a lot about you."

"I hope it wasn't too shocking," Dennis said.

Peter laughed. "Nothing worse than the things that I did when I was little." He winked at Arthur.

Arthur decided he liked this brother of Lydia's. "Can I see your violin?" he asked.

"I've just put it away," Peter said. "But I'm sure I'll be seeing you again and you can see it then. I'll be staying for a week. I have another concert here."

"You have to stay with us," Lydia said.

"I would love to," Peter said, "but I wouldn't want to be too much trouble for you." He looked down at Lydia's big stomach.

"Don't be silly," Lydia said. "I wouldn't let you stay anywhere else. You won't be any more trouble than Arthur, I'm sure."

"Well, that's a relief," Peter said. "I never did like hotels much."

They went out, Lydia clinging to Peter's arm. They talked the whole way home, about people Arthur did not know and places he had never been to. He began to feel sleepy, and he was glad when they got home.

Sunday afternoon Peter said he needed to practice. "I'll be in the guestroom for the next few hours," he said. "It won't bother you, I hope?"

"No," Lydia said. "At least you won't be practicing in the bathroom like you always did when we were young."

Peter grinned. "The acoustics were always better in there."

"What are acc – acc – those things?" Arthur asked.

"Acoustics? It's the quality a room has, what makes it easy or hard to hear something," Peter explained.

"Why do you have to practice?" Arthur wanted to know.

"That's how you get good, and stay good," Peter said.

"Can I watch you?"

"Arthur, I don't think that's a good idea," Lydia said quickly.

"I don't mind as long as you sit still and don't make a sound," Peter said.

Beaming all over, Arthur followed Peter into the guest room. He sat on the bed and watched as Peter took his violin out, tuned it, and started to play some slow scales. He played scales for half an hour, getting faster and faster. Arthur watched in spellbound fascination. Peter's fingers flew so fast, and his bow moved no slower. Arthur's desire to play that wonderful instrument grew even greater.

He sat in his corner until Peter had finished, three hours later. Arthur had never voluntarily sat still so long.

Peter turned around and smiled at him. "Would you like to try it?" he asked.

Arthur jumped up, a huge smile covering his face. Peter showed him how to hold the violin. It was smooth in Arthur's hands, and rather long for him. He put the bow on the strings and drew it across as he had seen Peter do. A faint, scratchy noise came from the violin. Distressed, Arthur looked up at Peter. "Did I break it?" he asked.

Peter laughed and knelt down behind him. "Here," he said, "this is how you do it." He put his hand over Arthur's on the bow and pulled it back and forth. The sound that came out was much better than the one Arthur had made. "You need to have more weight on the bow," Peter said. "Now you try it."

Arthur pressed down as hard as he could and moved the bow. Peter cringed. "Not that hard. Don't force it; let the weight of your arm fall on the bow. There, that's it!"

Arthur played all of the strings and even tried moving his fingers around. It did not sound much like music. As Peter was putting the violin away he said, "I wish I could play the violin like you."

"You could, you know," Peter said.

"Don't I have to be grown up?" Arthur asked.

"No," Peter said. "I started playing when I was six years old."

Arthur sighed. "Well, I guess I'm too old now."

"No, you aren't," Peter said. "You can start at any age. There are all sorts of sizes of violins. It will be a while before you can play at my level, though. It takes a lot of work and patience."

At dinner that night Arthur said, "I want to learn the violin."

"I don't know," Dennis said. "Remember when you took piano lessons last year?"

Arthur remembered. It had been a painful few months before the teacher had refused to teach him any longer. "But I didn't want to play the piano," he said. "I want to play the violin."

"We'll see," was all Dennis would say.

The next day, however, Peter brought home a small violin case. "Is that for me?" Arthur cried, jumping up and down in excitement.

Peter turned it over. "Hmmm. Well, I don't think it would fit anyone else," he said.

When Kip came over later, Arthur took out his new violin and showed it to him, and even played the few notes that Peter taught him. Kip was so impressed that he determined to ask his parents if he might play the violin as well. The next day Kip came over with his new violin, and Peter showed him how to hold it and play some notes. The result was that a cacophonous duet could be heard throughout the house for some time until Dennis told Arthur he was not to play his violin until he had some proper lessons.

Arthur was very sad when Peter had to leave. "Why can't you stay longer?" he asked as he watched Peter pack up his things.

"I have other engagements," Peter said. "And I have a job with the orchestra in Vienna."

"Is it a big orchestra?" Arthur asked, momentarily distracted.

"Yes," Peter said. He stopped packing and sat down beside Arthur on the bed. "Vienna is a wonderful place. There's always music everywhere. You walk down the street and you can hear music coming from nearly anywhere. It's the music capital of the world. I always knew I wanted to visit there when I was younger, and I never thought I'd actually live there."

Arthur's thoughts went back to the present calamity. "If you stayed, you could teach me the violin. You could help me get really good."

"But you have a teacher," Peter said. "Miss Eliot from the orchestra is going to teach you. She's very good."

Arthur sighed. "I guess so. But I'm going to miss you a lot."

Peter smiled. "I'll miss you too. But you can write letters to me, and I'll write back."

"Promise?"

Peter held out his hand. "I promise."

Arthur felt a bit better. He could be content with that until he was older and he could go to Vienna and visit Peter.

8

Adventure in the Woods

It was a fine, warm spring when it came around. Arthur and Kip were happy because it meant that they could play outside for a longer time after school. Lydia and Mrs. Mortimer were happy because their houses were quieter, and the boys were not underfoot all day.

One day in late March, Mr. Reid announced that since the weather was so fine they would go out the next day and have lessons and a picnic in the woods. He had already asked their parents, and they had all said that it was a good idea.

Arthur and Kip were immensely excited. In all of their years at school they had never had lessons outdoors, with a picnic at that. They both declared that Mr. Reid was the best teacher the world had ever known, and Mr. Mortimer said he was inclined to agree, since he was able to make Arthur and Kip behave in school. Lydia and Mrs.

Mortimer made them both splendid lunches. Arthur had sandwiches, pickles, hard-boiled eggs, and cookies. Kip had sandwiches, hard-boiled eggs, carrots, and a chocolate cupcake.

They arrived at school at the usual time, and Mr. Reid took role as usual. When that was done they gathered up their books and lunches and set out. They were going to the lake, Mr. Reid said. Mr. Reid walked at the head and the children all followed behind in any order they pleased. The sun was warm, and the birds were singing loudly. It was like a holiday even though they were still having lessons. Lessons outside were hardly lessons at all.

Kip decided he should be riding a horse into battle, and a big black charger at that. Arthur joined him on his fierce bay stallion, and soon there was a whole cavalry behind Mr. Reid. Mr. Reid even joined in, and shouted out orders to the army as they went along. When they got to the clearing in the woods by the edge of the lake where they were to have lessons, Mr. Reid let the boys run around for a few minutes. Then he called to them to dismount, and they sat in a big circle. Angel Lidden made a fuss about sitting on the ground (she was wearing a very frilly pink dress which Arthur and Kip thought was a silly thing to wear on a picnic), so Mr. Reid gave her his jacket to sit on. Mr. Reid called role again, and everyone was there, so they began lessons.

Mr. Reid took a ball out of his pocket and said, "Let's work on our poem first." He recited it through, and it sounded very grand out in the open air. Then he tossed the ball across the circle to Jimmy Chandler. "Now," he said, "toss it back to me and recite the first two lines." Jimmy did so, and threw the ball back to Mr. Reid. Mr. Reid threw the ball again and again, each time to a different student, until they had recited the whole poem. Arthur caught the ball on the last two lines and was pleased when Mr. Reid said, "Good job, Arthur."

It was all quite fun after that, Arthur and Kip found, even if it was still lessons. For math Mr. Reid told the children to collect a pile of small sticks and stones, and they had to multiply them. For grammar they acted out verbs, and when they worked on diagramming sentences they split into groups and were given a sentence. Each person was a word, and they had to figure out where they belonged on a line Mr. Reid drew in the dirt.

For geography they made a map of Europe on the ground out of sticks and little rocks. They had to name each country and its capital. They stood in two lines, and one person from one line named a country that Mr. Reid pointed to, and the other person from the other line had to name the capital of that country. Arthur was across from Angel Lidden. Mr. Reid pointed to a country, and Angel promptly said, "Austria." She looked at Arthur smugly as if to say, "You can't do it."

Arthur screwed up his face and thought hard. He jumped up as he remembered. "It's Vienna!" he cried. "It's Vienna! Peter lives there!"

Mr. Reid smiled and patted him on the shoulder. "That's right," he said. "Good job, Arthur. Can you tell us anything about Vienna?"

"Lydia's brother Peter lives there," Arthur said importantly. "He plays the violin. He says there's lots of music in Vienna. He says it's the music capital of the world."

"That's right," Mr. Reid said. "Many of the great composers were born or lived there."

Arthur made a face at Angel as they left the line.

History was the best lesson of all. They made costumes and props out of greenery and sticks and their jackets which they had shed very early on, and acted out scenes from their history book. It was a very good idea, they found, for pretending they were historical characters made them remember what those characters did even better than if they had read it from a book. They were rather disappointed when it was time for lunch.

Arthur and Kip ate quickly and sailed bark boats in the lake with their friends for the rest of the lunch hour. When lunch was over, Mr. Reid called them all back, and said it was time for science. He told them to pair up and go collect some interesting thing in the woods and bring it back so they could talk about it. "Go quickly," he said, "and don't go too far. I'll blow a whistle when time is up."

Arthur and Kip immediately paired up and hurried off to find their specimen. When they got into the woods, they found so many interesting things that they could not agree on what to bring back.

"We could bring back two," Arthur suggested.

"Mr. Reid didn't say we could," Kip argued. "He just said bring back *a* specimen. Let's go a little farther."

"All right." Neither of them remembered that Mr. Reid had said not to go too far. They walked farther and farther, looking all around for some interesting specimen.

Then they found the perfect specimen. It was a short piece of hollow log, and there was a big, old spider web stretched across its mouth. They picked the log up. It was not very heavy. They peered into both ends of the log to see if there were any spiders in it. They knew it would be a bad idea to take it if there were any poisonous spiders inside. Dennis said if you got bitten by a poisonous spider you could get very sick and even die, depending on what kind of spider it was. As they began to walk back with their log, Arthur told a story about a man who had been bitten on his arm by a poisonous spider, and his arm had swelled up so much that it was bigger than his body. This was of course only half true. There had indeed been a man bitten by a spider, but his arm had not swollen to such extreme proportions. It made Kip a little nervous, though, and he kept glancing down at the log as they walked.

After a while Arthur stopped and looked around him. "I think we're going the wrong way," he said.

"How do you know?" Kip asked.

"Well, we've been walking for a lot longer than it took us to get to the log, and there's no sight of the lake."

Kip looked around and realized that Arthur was right. The woods were getting thicker, and there was no sight of the lake. They turned around and started back the other way.

"I think we're lost," Kip said finally, when they did not reach the lake. They put down the log and stood looking around them, hoping for a sign that would show them the way back. They felt very small and alone then, and the woods seemed very big.

"Maybe we should yell, and they'll hear us," Arthur suggested. They did so, but there was no answer. They were silent again, until Arthur suddenly cried out, "Listen!"

"What?" Kip said rather crossly. He was feeling a bit frightened.

"I hear water running." Arthur started towards the sound. "A stream should lead to the lake, right?" Kip picked up the log and followed him. He stopped suddenly when Arthur gave a yell and disappeared.

"Arthur?" Kip called. "Arthur, where are you?"

There was a long silence during which Kip began to worry that his friend had been swallowed up by the earth. He had read about such things in stories, but had never before thought it could happen. He called again, and after a bit he heard Arthur's voice, coming rather faintly. "I'm here. I fell in the stream."

Kip approached cautiously until he came to the edge of a very deep ravine through which water was running. Arthur was sitting in the water. "Can you get out?" Kip asked.

Arthur started to stand up, but sat down hard again with a cry of pain. "My foot hurts," he said.

"I'll see if I can pull you out somehow." Kip looked around him and found a big stick. He held out one end to Arthur. "Here, hold onto this, and I'll pull you out." Arthur grasped the end of the stick and Kip pulled hard, but the stream bed was too deep, and Kip was not strong enough. He lost his grip and sat down hard. "Oomph," he said.

Arthur was starting to shiver. "It's cold," he said.

Kip looked around anxiously. He was really becoming frightened. He was afraid they would never be found, and that Arthur would freeze to death. He put his hands in his pockets and found an old cookie that had somehow been overlooked. He realized he was hungry then; lunch seemed a very long time ago. He pulled it out and dusted it off. He gave half of it to Arthur, and they sat munching in silence.

After a while, Arthur asked, "Do you think they'll notice we're gone?"

"They probably will," Kip said. "Mr. Reid notices everything, after all. And Angel would probably tell on us if he didn't."

Arthur laughed a little. "She probably would," he agreed. "Gosh, did you see her face when I got Vienna right?"

Kip doubled over with laughter. "She looked like she was going to have a fit," he crowed. "You really got her that time."

Their laughter died out, and they were silent again. "It's too bad we didn't get to show our specimen," Arthur sighed. "It's so nice."

"Maybe we can show it tomorrow," Kip suggested. "I'm sure Mr. Reid would let us, unless he's really mad at us."

"You know," Arthur began hesitantly, "you know, school isn't all that bad anymore."

Kip nodded. "I know. I used to hate it, but it's kind of fun now. Mr. Reid's much better than that old Miss Brentwood. He makes things so much more interesting."

Arthur nodded. "I wonder what they're doing now? I wonder if they're done with school."

Back in the clearing by the lake, Mr. Reid was getting worried when Arthur and Kip did not return with the rest of the children. He asked the others if they had seen Arthur and Kip. No one had. Finally Mr. Reid took the children back to the schoolhouse. He went to the principal's office and told Mr. Mortimer that the boys were missing.

Mr. Mortimer did not ask any questions. "I'm going to find Dennis Ramsay," he said. "I'll meet you out there."

Dennis was finishing up his shift at the hospital. He took off his white coat and followed Mr. Mortimer out to the clearing in the woods. Mr. Reid was waiting for them.

"I've been calling them, but they haven't answered," he said. "But now that you're here we can all look in the woods."

"All right, let's meet up here in half an hour," Mr. Mortimer said. The men split up and took different directions, calling the boys' names. It was getting dark when Dennis heard Kip's voice. He followed the sound and found Kip sitting by himself. "Where's Arthur?" Dennis asked anxiously.

"He's in the stream," Kip told him. "He fell in and hurt his foot. I can't get him out because the ditch is too deep."

Dennis knelt down at the edge of the ditch and saw a drooping, shivering Arthur sitting in the stream. "Oh, thank goodness," he said, his voice rather hoarse. He pulled Arthur out and wrapped his jacket around him. Arthur was shivering violently, and he could not walk. He took one step and fell down.

"I hurt my foot," he whispered as Dennis picked him up.

Dennis felt his forehead. "You're going to have a fever; we'd better get you home."

They went back to the clearing, met up with Mr. Reid and Mr. Mortimer, and went back to their cars. Kip explained what had happened.

"You should have listened to your teacher," Mr. Mortimer scolded.

Kip hung his head. "I'm sorry. We just wanted to find something really nice."

Mr. Reid patted his shoulder. "I'm just glad you're both safe. We won't say anything more about it. And I'll tell you what: when Arthur's better you can show the rest of the class your log. I'll keep it safe until then."

When they got home, Lydia helped Arthur out of his wet clothes and gave him a hot bath. Then Dennis looked at his foot. "It's a bad sprain," he said. "I'll wrap it up, and you'll have to stay off it for a week or two."

"A week or two!" Arthur groaned.

"You'll survive," Dennis said heartlessly. He felt Arthur's forehead. "Let's get you to bed now; you're burning up." He carried Arthur up to his bed and tucked him up with a hot water bottle. Lydia brought him a cup of chamomile tea.

Arthur was sick for four days. At the end of the fourth day he was able to sit up and drink some broth, and on the fifth day he could get up and sit on the sofa. He was glad to be up because he hated being sick; it was such a terrible waste of time. There were so many other, better things to be done that could not be done lying in bed. Dennis brought him a pair of crutches so he could get around. Arthur figured out how to get around on only one crutch, and he could pretend he was a pirate with a wooden leg. This made up for not being able to run around and play. And Lydia was very nice and made him all his favorite food. Miss Rachel brought over some cookies and stayed to talk. And of course Kip was over every possible moment.

As soon as Dennis said he was well enough, Arthur went back to school. Not much more than a month ago he would have complained, but somehow he was happy to go back to school. He and Kip were excited to show the class their scientific find, which Kip had stored safely in his tree house. As he dressed for school he thought that perhaps he would be a scientist when he grew up. Scientists could find so many interesting things. But as he put on his shoes he remembered that someone had said scientists needed to know a lot of math. Perhaps he should just stick with being a pirate after all. That way he could find lots of interesting things and not have to worry so much about math. But then he also wanted to be a professional violinist like Peter Benson. It was so hard to decide. Maybe he could be a pirate violinist. He supposed when you were on the high seas for months at a time some music would come in handy. That would do it. It was good to have one's future decided.

9

The Violinists

Arthur and Kip liked their violin teacher, Miss Eliot. She was young, and she was not at all mousy. When they had their lessons she sometimes made up games for them if they behaved. She was strict, but Arthur and Kip did not mind, because it was a kind strictness. She was not at all like Arthur's old piano teacher. Arthur's old piano teacher had been old and grumpy. She was always telling him to sit up straight, and she hit his fingers with a pencil if he did not get something right. She'd had a little white dog that barked at him and smelled terrible, and a big yellow cat that lay on the piano and looked at Arthur with evil eyes while he played. He had hated his piano teacher's house, too. It was always dark and gloomy, and it rather scared him. Miss Eliot did not own a single dog or cat. She lived in a sunny little apartment that was full of music. She had a big grand piano, several violins, a bigger violin called a viola, and lots of books of music. Her shelves were crammed full of music books. She even had framed music on the walls. They were very sloppily done, nothing like the tidy black notes in neat rows that Miss Eliot gave them to play. The framed music was scribbled over and inked out in places, and Arthur and Kip could hardly read the notes. Miss Eliot said they were copies of original manuscripts. She showed them her favorite. It was by Beethoven, she said: the violin concerto in D.

"Why, that's the one Peter played, isn't it?" Arthur said.

Miss Eliot nodded. "It is. I love that concerto. I wish I could play it half as well as Peter Benson does." She played a little bit for them, and Arthur and Kip thought she played it very well. Miss Eliot laughed and told them they were sweet, and gave them each a brownie.

Miss Eliot often had sweets for them when they finished their lessons. She was almost as good a cook as Miss Rachel, but not quite. She could be terribly absent-minded sometimes, and she often forgot she had put something in the oven to bake. Once, when Arthur was having his lesson and Kip was waiting, the whole apartment filled with smoke. They thought the building was on fire until Miss Eliot remembered she had put a pan of cookies in to bake and completely forgotten them. The neighbors did not know that, and they called the fire department.

It was a terribly exciting day. Three fire trucks came and started to squirt water on Miss Eliot's apartment until she ran out and told them what had happened. The firemen were not convinced at first, but when they finally realized what had happened, they all started laughing so much they could hardly stop. Miss Eliot said she was terribly sorry, and she wished she could give them something to make up for it, but all she had was unbaked cookie dough. One of the firemen said, "Well, I like cookie dough just fine. What kind is it?"

"Chocolate chip," Miss Eliot said weakly. "I'll go get it."

The violin lesson was forgotten that day. They all sat out on the lawn and ate cookie dough out of the bowl and laughed over the false alarm. One of the firemen said he had never had such a good false alarm before.

There were other mishaps, but none of them were quite as exciting as the burnt cookie incident. There was the time Miss Eliot was listening to a new record and did not notice she had taken down the salt canister instead of the sugar. When Arthur and Kip came for their lessons she brought out a lovely brown pan of brownies and cut them each a big piece. Arthur and Kip were very fond of brownies, so they both took big bites. Those bites did not stay long in their mouths, and Miss Eliot grew quite alarmed. She tried a piece herself and spat it out right away. "Gracious, what was I thinking?" she said. "This won't do at all. I'm dreadfully sorry, boys. I think I have some peppermints in the cupboard. Will that do?"

That did very well, though Arthur and Kip were sorry to have missed the brownies. The next week, though, there was another lovely pan of brownies, and this one had sugar in it, not salt.

One day when they came for their lesson, Miss Eliot looked excited. "I've had such a splendid idea," she told them. "I have several other students, and you are all doing so well that I would like to reward you. I was thinking of having a recital."

Arthur's heart immediately sank. Kip just looked blank. He had never played in a recital before, and he did not know too much about it.

"Do we have to?" Arthur asked.

"Wouldn't you like to?" Miss Eliot looked so excited that Arthur felt terrible about saying no.

"Well…" he said, "I guess it wouldn't be too bad."

"Wonderful!" Miss Eliot cried. "I thought I'd have it two weeks from now. Will you tell your families? I'll send them a notice soon, but I thought they'd like to know sooner."

As they walked home, Kip asked, "Why aren't you excited about the recital?"

Arthur groaned. "I had to play in a recital when I was learning how to play the piano. It was so dreadful. It was boring, and – and – you *have to play for people.*"

Even this last dreadful thing failed to make Kip understand. "I think it will be fun," he said.

"Just you wait," Arthur said dourly.

Later at dinner Arthur told Dennis and Lydia that Miss Eliot wanted to have a recital. Dennis and Lydia looked at each other. They remembered Arthur's last recital all too well. He had not misbehaved, but he had been so scared that he had forgotten his piece completely and just sat staring at the keyboard until his teacher led him offstage.

"I don't want to do it," Arthur said.

"We can help you this time," Dennis said. "You can play your piece for us, and for the Mortimers, until you are used to playing for an audience."

Arthur shook his head gloomily. "I don't want to. I want it to be a surprise."

"Well, all right," Lydia said. "You'll be fine, Arthur. I know you will."

But Lydia's encouraging words did not make Arthur feel any better. He went to bed with a sick feeling in the pit of his stomach. Maybe he had appendicitis, he thought. If he had appendicitis he would have to have his appendix out, and then he would have to rest for a long time, and he would not have time to practice, and he would not have to play in the recital. But he woke up the next morning feeling just as well as ever, and his appendix had not burst. It looked like he would just have to play in the recital.

Kip was still excited about the recital. As soon as school was over he said he had to go home and practice. He wanted to be very good for the recital. Arthur dragged himself home and half-heartedly took out his violin. He might as well practice, since there was nothing else to do. He just wished the recital was over and done with.

The next week at their lesson, Miss Eliot took one look at Arthur's long face and asked him what was wrong. "I can't play in the recital," Arthur mumbled.

"Why not?" Miss Eliot asked.

Arthur plucked his strings. "I'll forget," he said after a while.

"Forget what?"

"The piece."

"Why ever would you forget the piece?" Miss Eliot asked.

"Because I did last time." It stood to reason.

Miss Eliot smiled. "Oh, now I see what the trouble is. Well, perhaps I have a solution. Would you two like to play a duet?"

"What's a duet?" Kip asked.

"It's where two people play together."

"Like in an orchestra?" Arthur wanted to know.

"A little," Miss Eliot said. "But there are only two of you. Perhaps if you have someone playing with you, Arthur, you won't be as nervous, and you won't forget your piece."

"Maybe," Arthur said slowly.

"Why don't we try one," Miss Eliot suggested. "If you like it, then you can play it for the recital." She rummaged amongst her music books for a few minutes, and came out with a book. "Here it is. I played this duet with my own

94

friend when I was a little girl. It's very easy, and I think you'll like it. It's called 'Ode to Joy,' by Beethoven."

"Oh! Lydia likes that one," Arthur said. "She listens to it a lot on the record player."

"Well then," said Miss Eliot, "she'll be glad to hear you play it. Now, let's get started."

Arthur and Kip liked the duet. It was easy to play, and they liked the melody. When they had both learned their parts they tried to play them together. It was disastrous at first. Neither of them was particularly good at counting, and they could not stay together for more than a measure. But with Miss Eliot's help they could finally stay together half of the time.

"Now go home and practice it," Miss Eliot said. "And remember to count!"

Count they did. They counted and counted until the numbers got all mixed up and they had to stop. For a while it seemed like the two parts would never come together and sound like they should, but finally the day came when they were playing together, just as they should be. They were so excited that they started to whoop and jump around until they remembered that violins were delicate instruments and probably should not be jumped around with. They went back to practicing.

Then the day of the recital came. Arthur woke up feeling very nervous. He hardly ate any breakfast. Lydia understood, and she packed him a little extra in his lunch in case he got hungry later on at school. Arthur and Kip did not talk much on their way to school. Kip was finally feeling nervous. He had grasshoppers jumping around in his stomach, he said. Maybe they should not have asked Miss Rachel, Mr. Reid, and some of their friends from school to their recital. It would only make them more nervous to have more people there. But it was done, and they could not very well un-invite them. They had a very hard time concentrating in school, but Mr. Reid did not say too much about it. He seemed to understand that they were nervous about their recital.

After school Arthur and Kip went home and practiced some more until it was time for dinner, and after dinner they had to get ready for the recital. Lydia laid out Arthur's good suit and a new red-and-gold tie that she had made for him. "You look very nice," she said when he was dressed. "You'll be just splendid." Arthur wasn't too sure about that. He was so nervous that his stomach was starting to feel sick. He took several deep breaths as Miss Eliot had told him to do, but it did not seem to help. He felt just as nervous as before. He went downstairs and got a drink of water while he was waiting for Dennis and Lydia.

When Dennis and Lydia were ready, they drove over to the hall where the recital was being held. It looked very nice. Miss Eliot had put out some fresh flowers, and the chairs were set up facing the small stage. Arthur went backstage where the rest of the students were waiting. Kip was already there, also dressed in his best suit. There were three girls and one other boy besides Arthur and Kip, and they were also dressed up in their best.

Miss Eliot came in and called their attention. "I am very proud of you all," she said. "You have worked so hard, and I am sure your parents and friends are excited to hear you play. Now, are we all ready?"

Arthur and Kip said yes with the rest of the students, but they certainly did not feel ready. Their insides were jumping all over. They sat side by side on a bench backstage while the first few students went out to play. They were going last because they were the only ones playing a duet. Arthur wished they could go first and get it over with. It would be so much better if it were all over. He was afraid he would forget the music he had memorized, and everyone would be looking at him, and he would be so ashamed, just like at his piano recital. He chewed his thumbnail hard and tried to calm himself down. It did not work very well.

Finally it was their turn. They picked up their violins and followed Miss Eliot out onto the stage. Everyone in the audience clapped as they appeared. Arthur looked out into the audience, and it was a sea of faces. There were so many people! He felt very shaky.

Arthur and Kip bowed and stood together in front of the piano. Arthur could hardly hold up his violin, his hands were shaking so. Miss Eliot played the introduction to their duet. For an instant Arthur froze. He did not know what to do. He could not remember a single note. Then he looked up and saw them looking at him and smiling. They were all looking very encouraging and proud of him, Dennis, Lydia, Mr. Reid, the Mortimers, Miss Rachel. They knew he could do it, and suddenly he knew he could do it as well. He took a deep breath and he and Kip began to play. He remembered the notes. He remembered every single one of them, and he and Kip played together perfectly. They did not miss a single note, or get off at all. They finished their duet, and bowed as the audience cheered. It was very exciting. Miss Eliot called the rest of the students out, and they all took a bow together. The audience cheered so hard it was as if they were all professional violinists like Peter.

After the cheering had stopped, Miss Eliot thanked the audience and invited them to join the students for refreshments. The chairs were moved away, and tables were set out with all sorts of cookies and sweets. Miss Rachel had brought several different kinds of cookies, and Miss Eliot made a pan of her brownies. Arthur and Kip saw the two ladies exchanging recipes.

Arthur found his family, and Dennis and Lydia both hugged him and told him they were very proud of him, and he had done so very well. When they joined the Mortimers, Mrs. Mortimer hugged Arthur as well, and Mr. Mortimer shook his hand. Miss Rachel hugged them both and praised their "superb performance." "You'll be two more Peter Bensons yet," she said, "and I'll be proud to say that I gave you cookies when you were just Terrors on Two Feet."

Mr. Reid came and shook hands with them and told them it was some of the best violin playing he had ever heard. Arthur and Kip were pleased. Mr. Reid did not say things just to make you feel good. He always meant what he said. "I am very partial to Beethoven," he said, "and the *Ode to Joy* is one of his finest works. You did it justice."

Arthur did not quite understand what Mr. Reid meant by that, but he felt pleased all the same. As he went to get some cookies he felt very happy inside. He'd had a recital, and he had not forgotten his piece. He was on his way to becoming a real violinist, just like Peter Benson. Perhaps someday he would go to live in Vienna and meet a prince with a sword.

10

Dragon Hunting

In February Lent began. Lent was terrible because it was six long weeks without sweets. In Lent there were no calendars to open every day as there were in Advent, none of the mystery and excitement that led up to Christmas. But nothing lasts forever, as Lydia was fond of reminding Arthur, and soon there was only one week left until Easter.

Arthur was never quite sure what to make of the week before Easter. It was very solemn. And then there was Good Friday. Arthur still could not figure out why it was called "Good" Friday. Jesus died on that day, so it was not good, but Dennis said it *was* good, and how could dying be good? Dennis said he would come to a better understanding when he was older.

The Saturday before Easter was always a whirlwind of activity. On that day Lydia baked and cleaned, though this year she did not do as much because the baby was due any time. The Ramsays were all going over to the Mortimers for Easter dinner. That Saturday was also the day for egg decorating. Arthur and Kip spent the afternoon in Mrs. Mortimer's kitchen coloring hard-boiled eggs and decorating them.

That night Arthur took a bath and set out his Easter basket on the living room table, which was decorated with lilies and tulips. He had filled his basket with shredded green paper to look like a bird's nest. He liked his basket. It was very colorful. He'd had it ever since he was very little. His mother had bought it for him when he was a year old. His basket finished, he looked out of the window one more time to make sure it would not rain, and went to bed, thinking about the lovely treats his basket would be filled with in the morning.

Easter morning dawned bright and clear, with not a cloud in the sky. Arthur ran out to the hall, and there was his Easter basket, brimming with candy, a book, some model soldiers, and a rubber ball. He knew he was not allowed to eat any of his candy before breakfast, so he put it all carefully back.

Lydia called him to come get dressed. He went to his room and put on his best suit with a blue and gold tie Lydia had made for him. It was his favorite tie as far as ties go. When Dennis called that it was time to go they got in the car and drove to the church, which smelled of lilies. The big Easter candle was in a gold stand up by the altar.

Arthur was always awed by the Easter candle; it really was so very big. He thought that if he were an altar boy, he could carry it. He wondered how one became an altar boy. He would have to ask Dennis; Dennis had been an altar boy when he was young.

The Mortimers were already at church, and the Ramsays sat in the pew behind them. No sooner had they sat down when they had to stand up because the priest and the altar boys were processing in amidst a cloud of incense and a song. The candles and the long cross the altar boys were carrying looked even brighter today. Arthur wondered if they polished them extra specially for Easter.

When Mass was over, Arthur and Kip ran around outside the church while their families talked to friends. They passed by Miss Rachel, who wished them a happy Easter. They stopped to talk to her. Miss Rachel was one of the few grownups they enjoyed talking to because she did not talk to them like they could not understand anything.

"What are you doing today?" Arthur asked Miss Rachel. "Is your cousin coming?"

Miss Rachel shook her head. "No, she's not well. I'll be spending Easter by myself."

"Why don't you come to our house?" Kip suggested. "We're having a splendid dinner, and the Ramsays are coming."

"Oh, I wouldn't want to be a bother," Miss Rachel murmured.

"I'm sure you wouldn't be. I'll ask my mother." Kip dashed off and was back in a few moments with Mrs. Mortimer.

"Kip tells me you're spending Easter alone," Mrs. Mortimer said to Miss Rachel.

Miss Rachel nodded. "I was going to spend it with my cousin Maria, but she is not well."

"Well, you must come to dinner at our house," Mrs. Mortimer told her.

Miss Rachel murmured something about it being an imposition.

"You wouldn't be any trouble at all!" Mrs. Mortimer said. "You must come; I insist. We won't take no for an answer."

Miss Rachel smiled. "Very well, then. I would be happy to come."

Mrs. Mortimer smiled back. "That settles it then. We'll see you around two o'clock?"

Soon after that the two families went back to their houses for breakfast. Lydia made a grand breakfast. Besides eggs, sausage, and fruit, she had tried her hand at making the Easter bread. Dennis and Arthur's mother had always made it, and her mother before her. It was three strips of bread braided together with raisins inside and three hard-boiled eggs on top. Lydia's bread came out very well, and Dennis said it was delicious. Arthur thought so too; he had two large slices.

After breakfast, Arthur changed out of his church clothes and helped Lydia tidy up. When it was time to go, Lydia wrapped up another loaf of Easter bread and some salad she had made as her contribution to the dinner, and they walked over to the Mortimers' house. The house was decorated with lilies and tulips, and there were the eggs that the boys had made, as well as some very beautiful blown eggs that Kip's sister had made. They were called pysanky eggs, Kip informed Arthur, and Ukrainian people liked to make them. They were very hard to make. He had tried one, but it had not come out nearly as well as his sister's.

The Easter egg hunt came first. Arthur and Kip and Kip's little brother and sister had to stay inside the house and not look out of any of the windows while Mr. Mortimer and Dennis hid the eggs around the yard. Whoever got the most eggs would get a big chocolate rabbit as a prize, Mrs. Mortimer said. Arthur and Kip were both determined to find the most eggs and win the prize. The chocolate rabbit Mrs. Mortimer showed them was the biggest one they had ever seen.

When Dennis and Mr. Mortimer came back in from hiding the eggs, Arthur and Kip took the baskets Mrs. Mortimer gave them and rushed outside. Dennis and Mr. Mortimer had done a very good job of hiding the eggs, and it was a while before they found any. Arthur found a red one, and Kip found a green one and a blue one. Then Arthur found a very special egg. It was red, and it had his name on it in silver letters. But this egg was not hard-boiled like the rest; this egg was hollowed out with a big hole in one end, and out of that end stuck a whole dollar bill! Kip found his, a green one with his name on it, and they were so excited they almost forgot about finding the rest of their eggs. In the end they almost tied, Arthur ending up with one more egg than Kip. "Don't worry," he said to Kip as Mrs. Mortimer gave him the chocolate rabbit, "I'll give you half. We almost tied, after all."

After the egg hunt, they were not sure what they should do next. Mrs. Mortimer and Lydia were in the kitchen, talking and cooking. Mr. Mortimer and Dennis were on the front porch talking and drinking wine. The boys found both of those situations to be very dull, although the food did smell delicious. Miss Rachel arrived and gave the children each a little basket that she had made and filled with cookies and chocolates and little candy bird's eggs. They were very nice little baskets. The contents were even better. The boys ate some cookies and candy eggs while Miss Rachel went into the kitchen to talk and help cook. But even eating cookies and candy pales after a while, and they looked around for a new pastime.

"I know, why don't we look at my new book?" Kip suggested, and he brought it down from his room. It was a big book about St. George and the Dragon, and it had lots of lovely colored pictures. They sat on the porch steps and looked at the pictures together.

"I wish I was a knight," Arthur said.

"Me too." Kip looked at a picture of St. George on his horse, resplendent in his shining armor. "I bet it's better than being a pirate."

Arthur nodded. "Pirates don't have armor, or horses."

"Don't you think all that armor would get dreadfully hot?" Kip asked. "It must be something like an oven."

"It never says in any of the books," Arthur said. "Perhaps they made it special, so they wouldn't get hot. Otherwise I don't think so many knights would wear it. I wouldn't, if it were so hot."

"I suppose so," Kip agreed. "My book about knights doesn't say anything about armor being very hot, so I suppose it wasn't. Maybe they poked little holes all over it."

Arthur laughed. "Just like a sieve! I bet they got dreadfully wet when it rained!"

The thought was a comical one. The boys laughed hard as they imagined a knight wearing a very large sieve.

When they had stopped laughing, Arthur said, "I know! Let's play we're knights!"

"All right. I'll be St. George."

"But I want to be St. George!"

"I said it first! And it's my book!"

"So what? It was my idea to play knights!"

"Boys," Mr. Mortimer called down from the top of the porch. "No fighting."

They quickly lowered their voices. When adult attention was no longer directed at them, they began again in near whispers.

"Why don't you be the squire?" Arthur suggested.

"Squire!" Kip was scornful. "Why should I be the squire and you be St. George? It's not fair!"

"We can't both be St. George," Arthur said reasonably.

They glowered at each other until Kip had an idea. "I know! Why don't we neither of us be St. George. We can be different knights, and make up our own names. And then we'll go and kill a dragon."

Arthur considered this. "All right," he said. "I'm going to be Sir Percival."

"Who's that?" Kip asked.

"He's from a book about King Arthur that Dennis read to me," Arthur told him. "He was very strong."

"I want to be someone from the King Arthur book," Kip said.

"All right. You can be Sir Lancelot."

"That's a silly name," Kip scoffed.

"It is not! He was one of the knights of the Round Table."

"Aren't there any others?" Kip asked.

"Well…you can be Sir Gawain."

"What did he do?" Kip wanted to know.

"He fought a green knight," Arthur told him.

"A green knight? Who ever heard of such a thing? There's no such thing as a green knight."

"There is in King Arthur," Arthur said. "It's in the book."

"But people aren't green, unless they're sick. But I'm sure he wasn't sick all the time. Otherwise he wouldn't be able to fight."

"I think he was called green because he wore green armor, or something like that," Arthur said.

That made more sense to Kip. "Oh. Did he win? Sir Gawain, I mean, not the green knight."

Arthur nodded. "He beat him to smithereens."

That sounded just fine to Kip. Anyone who beat someone else to smithereens was all right as far as he was concerned. "All right, I'll be Sir Gawain," he said.

"Now we have to say the code of chivalry," Arthur said. "That's what all the knights do."

"What's that?" Kip asked.

"I don't know. It's just something they say. It's in the book. I'll get it." Arthur ran over to his house and got the book. He found the right page, and read it out loud: "'To never do outrage nor murder. Always to flee treason. To by no means be cruel but to give mercy unto him who asks for mercy. To always do ladies, gentlewomen, and widows suc – succor.'"

"What does that mean? Does it mean to kill girls?" Kip wondered.

"I don't know." Arthur called up, "Dennis, what does 'succor' mean?"

"It's an old word for 'help,'" Dennis said.

"Oh." Arthur turned back to the book. "I guess it means you have to help girls."

"Ugh." Kip made a face. "I guess it wasn't so great being a knight. Does it say anything else?"

"Let me see...it says 'to never force ladies, gentlewomen, or widows.' I guess that means you can't make them do anything. I guess they have to want to cook for you. The last thing is 'not to take up battles in wrongful quarrels for love or worldly goods.'"

"Why would you want to have a battle for love, anyway?" Kip wondered. "It's just silly."

"I happen to disagree," Mr. Mortimer called down from the porch.

"That's because you're married," Kip called back. They both wondered why Mr. Mortimer and Dennis laughed. It made sense to them.

"All right," Arthur said, "now let's get ready for battle." He had brought his own sword over along with the book. He and Kip went into the house and prepared themselves. They pinned pieces of cloth from Mrs. Mortimer's sewing basket around their shoulders and stuck their swords in their belts. In the books knights often had lovely ladies help them with their armor, but they did not need such things, especially since there were no lovely ladies handy. Though they were able to find enough for armor about the house, they were stumped when it came to helmets. They went to the kitchen to see if they could find anything.

"Here, I have some old bowls you can use," Mrs. Mortimer said. She dug two rather battered old bowls out from a cupboard. They fit nicely. The boys got some string and tied it around the bowls, and stuck feathers in the string. They were splendid helmets.

"Why, you look like proper knights," Miss Rachel said as they passed through. Arthur and Kip had to stop and be admired. They could not be rude to ladies; it was against the knight's code.

"Does that include Angel Lidden?" Kip wondered as they went out into the woods.

"Hmm. I don't suppose it does," Arthur said. "After all, she's not a lady. She's only a girl, and not a very nice one."

They mounted upon their great war horses and galloped out to the woods. There they met a very large and very ferocious dragon. It was one of those dragons that disguises itself to look like a prickly bush. They are the worst kind of dragon because they can catch you very much unawares, and they are very hard to kill. They have poisoned spikes that stick in you, and if you do not pull them out quickly they will travel to your heart, and you will die in agony. But Sir Percival and Sir Gawain were not afraid of any spiny bush-dragon, and they fought it valiantly, with many yells and stout blows of their trusty swords. The dragon breathed its fiery breath at them and shot out its poisonous spikes, but it could not kill the brave knights. Before long the great dragon lay dead at their feet. They cut off its head and carried it home, because it was time for dinner and they were very hungry. Dragon-hunting is hard work.

The dragon's head was admired by all the adults, and put in a place of honor above the mantle in the living room. Then they all sat down to eat around two tables that had been put together and covered with white tablecloths. Mr. Mortimer said grace, and Mrs. Mortimer and Miss Rachel filled everyone's plates. It was a splendid dinner. There was a great big juicy, pink ham, mashed potatoes, asparagus, green beans, rolls shaped like chicks with little raisins for eyes, artichokes, salad, stuffed eggs, and Lydia's bread. The grownups had wine, and Arthur and Kip were each allowed a small glassful mixed with water, which delighted them as they could pretend they were still Sir Percival and Sir Gawain at a feast to celebrate the defeat of the dragon.

Arthur and Kip ate until they could hardly hold any more. They still had room for dessert, though, which was fortunate. For dessert there was a great big cake shaped like a lamb that Miss Rachel had made. It was iced in white, and it had two candy eyes and a little candy nose. It was the best cake they had ever seen. It almost seemed a pity to eat it, but they ate it anyway, and it was delicious.

After dinner they all went out onto the porch. It was a very nice evening, and the stars were coming out. Arthur and Kip were too full to talk much. They sat on the steps and nibbled their candy.

"I like Easter," Kip said after a while.

"Me too," Arthur agreed.

They were silent again. The grownups were laughing on the porch. "That was a grand dragon we killed," Arthur said.

"A perfect dragon," Kip agreed. "I don't suppose we could kill such a good one again."

"Not until next Easter, at least," Arthur said. "I think it's an Easter sort of dragon."

They spent the rest of the time until the Ramsays left planning their next dragon hunt. It was a long way away, but traditions need a lot of planning.

11

Blood Brothers and a Puppy

On a fine Saturday morning, Arthur went to Kip's tree house and hallooed to be let in. The rope ladder was let down, and up went Arthur. He found his friend sprawled on the floor of the tree house, reading a large book.

"What's that?" Arthur asked.

"It's a book about Rob Roy," Kip said.

"Who's that?"

"Some man who lived in Scotland," Kip explained.

"It looks boring." Arthur did not like books that did not have a lot of pictures, and this book did not seem to have any at all.

"Some of it is," Kip said. "I skip over those parts and read the battle parts."

Arthur's interest was instantly caught. He sat cross-legged on the floor beside Kip. "Is he a soldier?" he asked.

"I think he's an outlaw," Kip said. "He doesn't like the king."

"Does he rob people?"

"Sometimes. He has a band of men, and they pillage and fight."

"Oh," Arthur said. He did not know what pillage meant, but he did know what fighting meant. "Let's play Rob Roy."

"All right," Kip agreed. "I'll be Rob Roy."

"I want to be Rob Roy!" Arthur protested.

"No, I should be Rob Roy," Kip said.

"Why?" Arthur demanded.

"Because I've read the book before and you haven't," Kip explained. "I know what to do, and you don't, because you haven't read the book. You can be one of my loyal henchmen."

"What's that?"

"Um, it's like a...soldier," Kip said. "Only a very special one."

This arrangement seemed reasonable. "All right," Arthur agreed. "Are we going to rob some people?"

"Not yet," Kip said. "First we need to become blood brothers."

"Blood brothers? How do you do that?"

"We each cut our wrists a little and put them together so our blood mingles."

"Why?"

"Because that's what they do in the book."

That was reason enough for Arthur. "What are we going to cut ourselves with?" Neither of the boys owned pocket knives. "I could get a kitchen knife."

"No," Kip mused. "That wouldn't work. We need something sharper so we can make a tiny little cut." He thought for a moment, then said, "Arthur, doesn't Dennis have any scalpels?"

"You mean those sharp little blades?" Arthur asked.

"Yes," Kip said. "Those would be just right."

"I'm not allowed to go into Dennis' office," Arthur said doubtfully.

"Couldn't you just borrow one?" Kip asked. "We'd put it right back. We can't become blood brothers without one."

"I guess I could," Arthur said, unwilling to let the chance of becoming a blood brother go. "Dennis is mowing the lawn, and Lydia's taking a nap."

"Well, hurry," Kip ordered.

Arthur hurried. He went to Dennis' office and pushed open the door. He tiptoed across the room to where Dennis kept his equipment and found the scalpels. Holding one carefully between his thumb and forefinger, he crept out of the office and ran back to the tree house.

Kip surveyed the scalpel with satisfaction. "That's perfect," he said. "Do you want to go first?"

Arthur shook his head. Kip took the blade and made a little slash above his wrist. He handed the blade to Arthur, who was suddenly looking a little pale. Arthur took the blade, closed his eyes, and poked at his wrist. A drop of blood appeared. The boys held their wrists together and said an oath that Kip read from the Rob Roy book.

"There," Kip said. "Now we're blood brothers, and if you ever break the oath, I can kill you. You can kill me too if I break the oath. Now we have to sign our names in blood. We'll have to cut ourselves a bit more." He got some paper and a pen made out of a feather and handed them to Arthur.

Arthur took the blade and gingerly began to cut again. He wrote his name on the paper, and handed the blade and the knife to Kip. Kip took the blade and slashed at his wrist. Suddenly there was blood all over the place, and Kip was clutching his wrist. Arthur snatched a bandana, tied it tightly around the gaping wound, and handed the pen to Kip. "Hurry and write your name," he said.

Kip wrote his name and said, "My arm hurts."

Arthur looked concernedly at the blood that was already staining the bandana. "Maybe we should go show Dennis." Normally he would not want Dennis to know about it, but Kip was not looking too good, and that was an awful lot of blood.

Kip nodded. He was feeling a little weak.

Dennis stopped the lawn mower when the boys came up to him. He took one look at Kip's hand, and without asking any questions hurried them inside. When he had cleaned the wound he told Kip he would need a few stitches. Kip looked very worried.

116

"Don't worry," Arthur told his friend. "Dennis is a very good doctor."

Kip did not seem consoled. He'd had stitches once before, and it had hurt. Dennis came back with his equipment and told Kip to lay his arm on the small table. While he was threading his needle he started to tell a story about when he was young and had tried to put stitches in his cat that had gotten hurt in a fight. He had used a spool of his mother's red thread because he thought it would look more exciting. At the first stitch, the cat ran away howling, pulling the whole spool of thread behind it. There was a horrible tangle of thread all over the place, and Dennis had to buy his mother a new spool of thread with his allowance.

Kip laughed hard at the story. When it was done, he asked, "Aren't you going to start?"

Dennis tied off the end of the thread. "It's all done," he said. Kip gaped at the neatly stitched wound. As Dennis began to put his things away he asked, "Now, would you two mind telling me what happened? Arthur?"

"Weeeell," Arthur began.

"Well?" Dennis repeated.

"Well, we were playing…"

"Playing what?"

"A game."

"I fail to see what sort of game would require you to cut yourselves up," Dennis said in a very unsympathetic voice. He turned to the cabinet where he kept his medical things.

Arthur sighed and said, "We were becoming blood brothers."

"You were *what?*" Dennis turned around and looked at the two boys.

"You know, like in *Rob Roy*," Kip explained.

"Oh, yes; go on." Dennis turned back to his work. His shoulders were making a funny sort of motion.

"Well," Arthur went on, "we cut ourselves so we could mingle our blood, then we wanted to write our names in blood, and we cut ourselves again, but Kip did something, and he got cut bad."

"What did you use to cut yourselves?" Dennis asked.

Arthur looked at his feet. "Um, we used one of your scalpels."

"Arthur!" Dennis sounded very angry. "I have told you never to touch those! What were you thinking?"

Arthur kept his eyes on his feet. He knew he was not allowed to touch Dennis' things. He wished the floor would open up and he could crawl away and never be seen again.

Kip quickly came to his defense. "It was my idea. We were going to use pocket knives at first, but I thought that wouldn't work very well. I asked Arthur to get a scalpel for me."

Dennis sighed and sat down. "Arthur," he said, "I really ought to punish you for this, but I can see you've both been scared enough. Now listen to me," he went on in a serious tone, "you are never to play with any kind of knife again, especially my scalpels. It's very dangerous, and if I hadn't been around something bad could have happened to Kip. Will you promise me?"

The boys nodded, and Dennis nodded too. "All right," he said. "Now Kip, I'm going to take you home and explain to your mother what happened. You'll have to rest that hand for a while. Arthur, you can stay here and wait for me. While I'm gone I'd like you to wash your cut well with soap and water and put a bandage on it. When I get back we're going to have another talk about my office being off-limits."

Arthur sighed. He could see his Saturday flying away before his eyes. Whenever Dennis had a talk with him it was usually followed by some sort of chore. When Dennis came back he listened resignedly as his brother talked about how his work was to help people, and if Arthur played with his equipment then he could not help people when they were sick or hurt. Dennis finished with, "Now I don't want to say this again, understand?"

Arthur hung his head. "I'm sorry. I won't do it again."

Dennis nodded. "Kip won't be able to play any more today, so why don't you come help me finish the lawn. You can rake up."

At least he did not have to do something inside with Lydia. It was much better being outdoors, and cut grass had such a wonderful smell. Perhaps Dennis would let him

119

have the grass cuttings, and he and Kip could jump in them when Kip was better.

When they were done with the lawn, Arthur went inside to get something to eat, but the mail had come, and there was a letter for him from Peter, which made him forget about food for the moment. He took it out onto the porch to read it. Peter's letters were always very interesting, and Arthur was always excited to receive one. He had just played a concert, Peter said, and a prince had come to the concert. The prince, he said, was a very grand person. He was dressed in velvet and satin, and had a lot of medals on a sash across his chest. He had sat in a box with some very grand looking ladies in lovely gowns. Arthur did not really care about the ladies. He was much more interested in the prince's sword. Imagine being able to carry a real sword around! That would be wonderful. Peter enclosed a picture of the prince, cut out from a newspaper. He really did look grand, Arthur thought. He had never seen a real live prince before. Maybe when he was older and went to visit Peter in Vienna he could see the prince. Maybe the prince would even let him hold his sword. That would be grand. He couldn't imagine anything better.

Arthur put the letter away in the box he kept his letters from Peter in, and as his stomach was protesting loudly, he went to the kitchen in search of something to eat. Lydia gave him an apple and told him to go play outside. She was baking a peach pie and did not want to be disturbed. Pie-baking was always tricky for Lydia, and though she was getting better at it she needed to concentrate and not be bothered.

Arthur took his apple and went outside. He wandered down the street, munching and surveying everything around him with a bored air. It was never quite the same without Kip. It was a rather quiet afternoon. Miss Rachel was on her porch, sweeping as usual. Arthur walked over and sat on her steps.

"Where's your other half?" Miss Rachel asked.

"He got hurt," Arthur said. "He had to go home."

"Oh my," Miss Rachel said. "I hope it was nothing serious. What happened?"

"He got cut."

"By what?"

"A scalpel."

"That must have been some very bad doctor," Miss Rachel said. "I'm sure it wasn't your brother."

"No, it was me," Arthur said.

"You!" Miss Rachel put down her broom and sat down on a porch chair. "Why don't you tell me about it? This sounds quite exciting, if not a little macabre."

"What's 'macabre?'" Arthur asked.

"It means it is disturbing because it has to do with death or injury," Miss Rachel explained. "Here, have a cookie."

Arthur took a sugar cookie and between bites told Miss Rachel of the day's events. Miss Rachel had a very funny look on her face, almost as if she were trying not to laugh, but of course that was not it, because who would laugh at such a thing? People did not laugh when other people got hurt, unless it was in the cartoons, and those were not real. Besides, Miss Rachel was too nice to laugh at other people's misfortunes. She must have just smelt something funny, Arthur decided. She had a very sensitive nose.

"It looks like I'll have to bring some cookies over to young Master Kip," Miss Rachel said. "It seems he had an awful time of it."

"I had a very awful time too," Arthur said hopefully.

Miss Rachel laughed. "Oh, I'm sure you did, Tot Feet. Here, then, have another cookie. Goodness, I never thought I'd see the day when there was not only one Terror on Two Feet but two on this street. Now we have trouble squared."

Arthur took another cookie, waved a careless goodbye to Miss Rachel, and sauntered off down the sidewalk again. The street really was quiet at the moment. It was too bad Kip could not play. Arthur hardly knew what to do without his friend. He went down to the Lot. It too was deserted. Arthur wondered where everyone was. Perhaps they were all asleep, even though it was the middle of the afternoon. Sometimes people did that, though he could not understand why. He would rather be up and doing things during the day, especially when that day was a Saturday, with no school.

He sat on the swing and swung back and forth for a while in a lazy sort of way. When he grew tired of that he took out the ball from his Easter basket that he often carried around in his pocket and tossed it around. But it was not much fun without Kip to catch it, so he put it back in his pocket. He swung again, whistling a song.

It was while he was whistling his song that he thought he heard the sound. It was not a normal Saturday afternoon sort of sound; it made him stop and listen. He did not hear anything, so he went back to swinging and whistling. He was about to go and find other occupation when he heard it again. It was a whimpering sort of sound, and it was coming from a clump of bushes at the edge of the Lot. He picked up a stick and went to investigate.

It was a puppy, a tiny little Cocker Spaniel puppy. Arthur knew what kind of puppy it was because he had a book about dogs, and it looked like the pictures of the Cocker Spaniels. The puppy looked very sad, but it started jumping around and barking a shrill little bark when it saw Arthur. Arthur knelt down and coaxed it to him. He had a bit of crust in his pocket, and he gave it to the puppy. It gulped the crust up, and barked some more. Arthur petted it. It was very soft. Someone must have abandoned it, he thought. Puppies do not get lost. People just don't like them so they throw them out. Arthur wondered if he would be able to keep it. He would love to have a dog. He had never had his own dog before. They'd had a dog, years ago, before they had moved to Nightingale Lane, but she had been very old, and she had died. Arthur had loved her, but she was not much fun. A puppy would be a lot of fun. One could run around and play with a puppy. He must take the puppy home and show it to Dennis and Lydia. They would have to let him keep it.

He scooped the puppy up, and it settled into his arms with a little contented puppy sigh and began to lick his hand. Arthur started home, thinking about what he would call it. He could think of a lot of good names. He would have to get Kip to help him pick one.

He was almost to the street when someone yelled, "Hey!" He turned around to see a boy glaring at him. The boy was bigger than him, and his clothes were rather shabby. Arthur had never seen him before; he certainly did not live on Nightingale Lane.

"Hey!" the boy called again. "Hey you! I want that dog."

"But I found him," Arthur said.

"I don't care. You'd better give him to me."

Arthur held onto the dog. "Does he belong to you?" he asked.

The boy stopped and looked at him in surprise. "No…"

"Well, I'm keeping him," Arthur said stoutly. "You can't have him." He turned to go again, and was startled when the boy ran up behind him and pushed him. Arthur put the puppy in an old barrel that stood nearby and turned to face the boy. He had never been in a fight with such a big boy before, but he was determined to keep the puppy. And who knew what such a mean-looking boy might do to a little dog?

The boy rushed at him, his fists up. Arthur punched him as hard as he could. The boy roared in surprise and punched Arthur in the nose. It hurt terribly, and for a moment Arthur saw stars, just like in the books. He came back to consciousness immediately. Though his nose was bleeding ferociously, he fought back as hard as he could. They were rolling around in the dirt, lost in the throes of a ferocious battle, when someone pulled them apart. The strange boy got up and ran away. Arthur got up and rubbed dirt out of his eye. "Hello Mr. Reid," he said.

Mr. Reid took a handkerchief out of his pocket. "Here, clean yourself up a bit. I have an idea it wouldn't do to come home looking like this. That was some fight. I happened to be passing by, and I heard your sounds of strife. What was it about?"

Arthur wiped his face and handed the handkerchief back to Mr. Reid. "Here, I'll show you." He went to the barrel and lifted out the puppy. "I found him in the bushes, and that boy wanted him but I wouldn't let him."

Mr. Reid scratched the puppy behind the ears. "I can see why you were fighting so hard. He's a very fine puppy. He must belong to someone."

"I don't think so," Arthur said. "He must have been abandoned. I hope he is, because then maybe I can keep him."

"He would make a very good dog," Mr. Reid agreed. "Come on, I'll walk you home, in case that boy is still around."

As they walked to his house, Arthur began to feel very tired and rather achy. He could still taste blood in his mouth, his nose, his lower lip, and his left eye hurt, and he had scraped his elbow badly. His eye was starting to swell up and he could hardly see out of it. He had never been in such a bad fight before. Not that he had been in many fights at all. He had only been in one fight before this, at his old school. After that one Dennis had told him he did not want him fighting anymore, so Arthur had not, until now. He wondered what Dennis would say. He would probably be angry, especially after the afternoon's events.

Dennis was not angry, even after Mr. Reid had gone. He admired the puppy, said they would talk about it later, and sent Arthur up to take a hot bath. Arthur was very glad to take a bath. The hot water hurt his elbow where it had been scraped, so he kept it out of the water as best he could, but the water felt good on the rest of him.

After his bath he went back downstairs. Lydia had made a little bed in a basket for the puppy, and he was asleep in it. "I gave him some milk for his supper," Lydia said. "He was very hungry."

Dennis ruffled Arthur's hair. "You've had quite a day, haven't you, youngster?" he said. "Come into my office and I'll take care of those wounds."

Arthur watched as his brother cleaned and bandaged his elbow. "Dennis, can I keep the puppy?" he asked.

Dennis swabbed something stinging onto the scrape, making Arthur wince. "Yes, you may, if he doesn't belong to anyone."

"Can I really?" Arthur said excitedly. "Ow!" he added as Dennis swabbed some more stuff on his elbow.

Dennis smiled. "Hold still. Yes, really. It's been a long time since we've had a dog, and every family needs one. We'll start asking around tomorrow. Just don't get your hopes up, Arthur. He's a very fine puppy, and someone's sure to be looking for him."

Arthur's hopes were already up, but he did not worry. He knew, deep inside him, that the puppy was his. There was no other possibility.

"All right," Dennis said as he fastened the bandage, "that's that. Now, Lydia has some pork chops waiting for us, and there's a peach pie afterwards."

Arthur felt very contented as he went down to dinner. It had been a very eventful day, but it was good all the same.

12

Of Camping and Babies

I t was Arthur and Kip's birthday. Their birthdays were two days apart, and their families had decided to celebrate them together on one day. The Ramsays had dinner at the Mortimers', finishing it off with a splendid cake and ice cream and presents, and now they were all outside. It was getting dark, and a few crickets were singing because it was spring. The grownups sat on the porch and talked. Arthur and Kip lay on the grass and talked. It had been a splendid meal, and they were all feeling stuffed and lazy, so much so that no one mentioned it was getting near Arthur and Kip's bedtime.

Arthur's new puppy lay beside him, his fat little stomach moving up and down as he slept. Arthur and Dennis had put up "found" signs all over town. They had put an advertisement in the newspaper. They had even asked people if they knew of anyone who had lost a little

Cocker Spaniel puppy. No one knew of anyone who had lost a Cocker Spaniel puppy. And no one came to claim the puppy. So Dennis said that the puppy belonged to Arthur. Arthur was not surprised; he had known the puppy was his from the moment he saw him. But he was very happy all the same. He and Kip talked about it, and they decided that Sam would be a good name for the puppy.

From their recumbent position on the grass, the boys could see the first star coming out. They both made wishes. "I wonder how many stars there are?" Kip said.

"A billion and one, I suppose," Arthur replied.

"Why a billion and one?"

"Because new stars are always being born."

"Oh." Arthur's logic was somewhat to be wished for, but to the workings of Kip's mind it made sense.

"I would like to count all the stars," Arthur went on. "We couldn't really see the stars where we lived before, because we were in the city, and there were too many lights. Have you ever done it?"

"No," Kip said. "I mean, I tried to once, but I lost count. Jerry says it's silly to try, because it's impossible."

"What does Jerry know?" Arthur scoffed.

"Nothing." Kip was fond of his older brother, but siblings can be very unfathomable sometimes.

"Have you heard of supernovas?" Arthur asked.

Kip shook his head. "What are they?"

"Dennis told me about them," Arthur said importantly. "You see, there are these stars called white dwarfs – they're the kind of middle-aged stars. They explode, and that's called a nova. When they explode really big they're called supernovas. They get colorful from all the dust that comes from them. I saw a picture of one once. It was really amazing."

Kip was suitably impressed by Arthur's store of knowledge, after which they were silent for a time. Suddenly Kip said, "I wonder what it would be like to sleep under the stars? I've never done it. Have you?"

Arthur shook his head. "Dennis took me camping once when I was seven, but we slept in a tent."

"Me too." They were silent again, both imagining a night sleeping under the stars with a fine campfire. It was just the sort of thing they would like to do, but at the present was just a dream.

Kip sat up. "I know, why don't we camp out sometime? Just us two, I mean."

"They probably wouldn't let us," Arthur said doubtfully. "They'd probably say we're not old enough."

"They don't need to know," Kip said. "We could sneak out after bedtime. We could build a little campfire."

Arthur became excited. "Let's!" he agreed. "Where shall we go?"

"We can go in the little forest behind the house," Kip suggested. "It would be a perfect place. There's that little clearing where we could build a fire. There's a fire pit there where we roast things sometimes. It's quite safe."

While they made their plans the grownups talked on the porch, quite unaware of the machinations of the schemers. They decided on the next night. That way they would have time to gather supplies and store them in the tree house.

Just as they were finishing with their plans, Dennis called, "Arthur, time to go in." The boys walked up to the porch, and they heard Mr. Mortimer say, "I really don't think he'll come here. Greenwich is quite a distance from here, and they'll be bound to catch him before he has time to get here."

"I certainly hope so," Dennis said. "We don't need any trouble of that sort around here."

"It's an escaped criminal," Kip whispered to Arthur. "I read about it in the newspaper. He's terribly dangerous. He's already shot ten men dead, one right after the other." This was a gross exaggeration; the man had only shot and wounded one man on his way out, but all the same it was a daring feat, and Kip was impressed enough to make it ten men instead of one.

The boys parted for their respective beds with whispered reminders of the following night.

They thought that the next night would never come, but it did. At nine o'clock Arthur was ready and willing to go to bed, such a rare occurrence that Dennis asked if he was feeling well. As soon as it was safe, Arthur crept out of bed, pulled on his clothes, and climbed out of the window. He met Kip at the tree house, and they quietly gathered up their equipment and lugged it to the chosen campsite.

It was an ideal spot. The fire ring was there, just as Kip had said, and it looked quite safe. Since there were no trees overhead they could lie on their backs and look at the stars to their hearts' content. They built a small fire and cooked some sausages that Kip had taken from his mother's kitchen. There was nothing better than roasted sausages, they both decided. Unless it was ice cream. There was no need to, but they talked in whispers. After a while they got into their sleeping bags.

"Look at the stars," Kip whispered. "Aren't they bright?"

Arthur nodded. "There are so many. Gosh, I don't think I've ever seen so many all at once."

"There was a long, contented silence, then Kip whispered, "Goodnight, Arthur."

"Goodnight," Arthur whispered back. He gave a small sigh and settled into his sleeping bag. Soon both boys were asleep.

An hour later, Kip's brother went up to bed and noticed Kip's bed was empty. He thought nothing of it, supposing Kip had gone to the bathroom or to get a drink of water, but when half an hour had passed and still there was no Kip, Jerry grew a little worried. He went downstairs and asked his parents if they had seen Kip.

"Did you check in the bathrooms?" Mrs. Mortimer asked.

Jerry nodded. "He's not in any of them."

Mr. and Mrs. Mortimer went up to Kip's room to take another look around. The window was open, but that was not unusual, as Kip often slept with his window open. He was still not there, so a search of the house commenced. Jerry went out and looked in the tree house, but Kip was not to be found.

"Oh dear," Mrs. Mortimer said worriedly.

Mr. Mortimer said something that the female members of his family discreetly ignored, and went to fetch a flashlight. "I'll have another look around outside," he said. He went outside and called Kip's name several times, but there was no answer. Then he smelt smoke. It seemed to be coming from the woods. He hurried to the Ramsay's house and knocked on the door.

Dennis came to the door in answer to his knock, his shirt untucked and his feet bare. "Why, hello Henry," he said. "Is something wrong?"

"Is Arthur in his bed?" Mr. Mortimer asked. "Kip's missing."

"I'll go check," said Lydia. She came down in a few moments with a worried look on her face. "He's not there," she said. "And his window is open. It wasn't when he went to bed."

"I noticed smoke out in the woods," Mr. Mortimer was telling Dennis. "I don't know if it's them or not, but we should check it out."

Dennis also said something indecorous. "Let me get some shoes on, and I'll meet you outside," he said to Mr. Mortimer.

In a few minutes the two men met outside. Mr. Mortimer was pushing a pistol into the belt of his trousers. "Why the pistol?" Dennis asked.

"It never hurts to be careful," Mr. Mortimer said grimly. He and Dennis made their way through their backyards and into the woods with the help of their flashlights. The smoke seemed to be coming from a clearing ahead. They approached cautiously. A fire was burning low, and in the strange shadows it cast they could see a long figure in a sleeping bag lying beside the fire.

They drew back a little. "Do you think it's...?" Dennis whispered.

"I don't know," Mr. Mortimer said. "I don't think he could have made it in so short a time, but you never know. Desperate people can do very desperate things."

The figure in the sleeping bag sat up at that moment. All the two men saw was hair, and something that looked like a gun. Mr. Mortimer instantly pulled the pistol out of his belt and called, "Don't move, or I'll shoot."

The figure jumped up. Just in the nick of time, Mr. Mortimer managed to point the pistol away so that it went off into the trees. He dropped the pistol, took the figure by the shoulders, and shook it. "Christopher-Paul," he cried, "what are you doing? Don't you realize I could have killed you?"

"But you didn't," Kip said reasonably. He was quite surprised when his father gave him a sound slap on his bottom.

"Where's Arthur?" Dennis demanded.

"Here I am." Arthur popped out from the end of the sleeping bag. "Hi Dennis." He wondered why his brother and Mr. Mortimer looked so terribly pale in the firelight. "Somebody shot," he said. "Or maybe it was a dream."

"It wasn't a dream," Dennis said grimly. He took Arthur firmly by the arm. "You are going to have a lot of explaining to do, but in the morning. Right now you're going straight home to bed."

"You too, young man," Mr. Mortimer said to his son.

Arthur and Kip, under Mr. Mortimer's stern direction, gathered up their things while Dennis put out the fire. Then they all went home. They boys felt rather dejected that their night under the stars had been cut short, and they knew they were in big trouble. They could not quite understand why. It wasn't as if it was terribly wrong to sleep out under the stars. Lots of people did it.

When Arthur and Dennis got home, Lydia hugged Arthur, and then shook him. "You had me worried half to death," she said. "Now go to bed, and *stay* there."

Arthur went to bed. He did not want to feel any more of Dennis' wrath. He would certainly get enough of that in the morning.

Arthur woke to Dennis calling his name. He rolled over and murmured sleepily, "Is it morning?"

"No," Dennis said. "Lydia's having her baby. I'm taking her to the hospital, so I want you to go over to the Mortimers' and stay there until I come for you."

Arthur stumbled out of bed and ran into his dresser. Dennis grabbed his shoulder and steered him clear. "Here, this way. I guess I'd better give you a ride on my back over to the Mortimers'." He wrapped Arthur's arms around his neck and lifted him up. Arthur yawned and fell asleep again.

He did not wake up again until the sun was shining in at the window. He opened his eyes and looked around. He was in Kip's room, and for a moment he wondered how he came to be there and not in his own bed at home. Then he vaguely remembered that he and Kip had tried to camp out in the clearing, and they had been discovered and brought back, and he had gone to sleep in his own bed, but Dennis had woken him up and brought him over to the Mortimer's for some reason. What was it again? He racked his brain hard to remember. Oh yes, that was it! Lydia was having her baby, and Dennis had taken her to the hospital. He wondered why she had to go to the hospital. She was not sick; she was just having a baby.

Kip woke up and rubbed his eyes. He looked at Arthur without surprise, and then suddenly let out a yelp. "Oh!" he said. "You're here!"

"Lydia's having her baby," Arthur explained. "Dennis had to take her to the hospital, so he brought me here last night."

"That's super!" Kip exclaimed. He sat up and said, "Do you remember our camp-out last night?"

Arthur nodded. "It's too bad they stopped us. I guess we're in a lot of trouble. They seemed pretty mad."

"Maybe since Mrs. Ramsay is having her baby, they've forgotten about it," Kip suggested hopefully.

Arthur brightened. "Yes, perhaps."

Kip's parents had not forgotten Arthur and Kip's escapade, however, even if Dennis and Lydia had other things on their minds. But Mr. Mortimer was not ready to do anything about it yet. As the boys sat down to breakfast, he fixed a stern eye on the two of them and said, "Don't think we've forgotten about your little escapade last night. But in light of the present circumstance, I will postpone the discussion of your misdeed until such a time as is more fitting."

The boys stared at him blankly. "Let me rephrase," Mr. Mortimer said. "Since Mr. and Mrs. Ramsay are at the hospital and otherwise occupied at the present, we will talk about this later. But I am sure Mrs. Mortimer needs help with something this morning."

During breakfast Dennis telephoned and said that Lydia had a baby girl, and they were both doing very well. Arthur wondered why Lydia had to have a girl. Girls really were not good for much, and this little girl was sure to be bossy; all girls were. Dennis said Arthur was to stay at the Mortimers' one more night, and he and Lydia would be home the next morning.

The next morning they did indeed come back, and with them was the new baby. Lydia sat down on the sofa and unfolded the blanket so Arthur could see. She was very tiny, and she was very pink. She had only a very little bit of hair on her head, and it was dark. She was sleeping, and her tiny hands were curled up in little balls.

"Would you like to hold your niece?" Lydia asked.

"I don't know," Arthur said. "I might drop her."

"Don't worry," Lydia said. "Here, sit down, and then you won't drop her." Arthur sat on the sofa and Lydia lifted the little bundle of baby into his arms. Arthur sat very still and looked at the baby. "Does she have a name?" he asked.

"We were thinking about calling her Alice, after our mother," Dennis said. "What do you think?"

"It's a nice name," Arthur said. He looked at the baby again. At that moment she opened her eyes and looked straight up at him. Her eyes were blue, like Lydia's. She opened one of her tiny hands and waved it around. Arthur decided she was not so bad after all, even though she was a girl. Besides, he was her uncle and he had to look out for her. It was what uncles did. It was a rather nice thing being an uncle, he decided.

"Hello, Alice," Arthur said.

13

Arthur and Kip to the Rescue

It was rather nice to have a baby around the house, Arthur decided as the days went by. Alice was a very fascinating creature, when she was awake. She was so very tiny. Arthur had never seen such a tiny human being before. Alice was a very quiet baby, and she hardly ever cried. She was very smart, too. When Arthur talked to her she looked as if she could understand him, and if he moved his finger around she could follow it with her eyes. She made such funny noises when she was happy. Arthur found that if he tickled the bottoms of her tiny feet she would wiggle herself around and almost laugh. Lydia had a baby carriage for her, and when she took Alice out for a walk she would let Arthur push her as long as he was careful and did not jolt her too much. Arthur felt very proud when he was out pushing his little niece in the baby carriage. She really was such a nice looking baby. He had never seen such a nice looking baby before. All the other babies he had known were ugly and red and cried a lot.

The only trouble with having a baby around the house was that Arthur had to be quiet when she napped. And she napped a lot. Arthur could not understand it. Why would anyone want to sleep as much as that baby did? Of course, Alice was very small, and there was not much she could do besides eat and lie around and kick her legs. She could not even eat good things like cookies and apples and pickles. Arthur decided it must not be very fun to be a baby. It was hard to imagine that he himself had once been so tiny and unable to do things. It was much nicer being eight years old. He couldn't wait until Alice got bigger and he could do things with her that did not just involve pushing her around in a baby carriage. Alice would not be one of those sissy girls that dressed in frilly pink dresses and hated to run around and get dirty. Arthur would teach her everything he knew. He would teach her how to climb trees, how to catch frogs and lizards, how to fight with a sword. He would teach her not to scream when she saw a mouse or a spider. He would teach her how to make paper boats and sail them in the stream. She would be the best girl ever. Arthur felt that he had a duty towards his young niece. Those were the sorts of things uncles should do, he decided, and he would not lack in any of his duties as an uncle. He would be the best uncle in the world.

He did not realize how soon he would have to be the best uncle in the world.

It all began on a warm, sunny day in June. School was out, and Arthur and Kip were free. They were so delighted with their newfound freedom that they hardly knew what to do. But it was the sort of day that begged for adventures. They did not yet know what kind of adventures; they would have to go out and seek them. It was a surprise-adventures sort of day. They went and said hello to baby Alice, who was just getting ready for a nap. Then they walked down the street, talking about nothing in particular. It was just the sort of day to walk down the street and talk about nothing in particular.

They passed by Angel Lidden's house. Angel was sitting on a bench under a tree, reading a book. She was dressed, as usual, in a silly, poufy dress, the kind of dress that would not stand up to any sort of thing that was in the least bit fun. Arthur and Kip stopped to stare at her. They could not understand why she would be reading a book on a day that just begged for adventures. They were not against reading books; they had many books that they liked to read. But there were days for reading books, and there were days for seeking adventure. Today was a day for seeking adventure, and there Angel Lidden sat, reading. Angel ignored them as they stood and stared at her. She sat very still and straight, and read her book. The boys wanted sorely to throw something at her, but they both knew they would get in trouble if they did, and it was not the sort of day for getting in trouble.

So they were quite delighted when they saw a very large caterpillar crawling down a branch of the tree above Angel. They clasped their hands together and hoped and wished that it would happen. And it did. They could not have planned it any better. Angel was very calmly turning a page of her book when the caterpillar wobbled on the branch. It leaned to one side, then to the other, and then it fell. It fell straight onto Angel's lap.

A piercing scream shattered the peaceful neighborhood. Angel jumped up, waving her hands in the air and screaming bloody murder. Arthur and Kip watched and laughed. Angel's mother came running out to see what was wrong with her precious child. The first culprits she saw were Arthur and Kip. She rushed at them, crying, "You terrible boys! You get away from my Angel! Your parents will hear about this! How could you?"

Arthur and Kip did not care. They both knew they hadn't done a thing. It was an act of God as far as they knew. A perfectly wonderful act of God. They smiled at each other contentedly and wandered off down the street.

Miss Rachel was on her porch, sweeping as usual. She stopped and rested her broom against the porch railings as the boys came up. "Why, it's the Terrors on Two Feet," she said. "What have you been doing to Angel Lidden now?"

"Nothing," Kip said, sitting down on the porch steps and accepting the cookies that Miss Rachel offered to him. "Nothing at all. It was simply wonderful, though. We were just standing there minding our own business when a wonderful huge caterpillar fell out of the tree."

Miss Rachel raised her eyebrows. "Fell out of the tree, you say? Hmm."

"It did," Arthur said. "Right out of the tree. We didn't have a thing to do with it. It was pretty great."

"Well, I hope for your sakes that your elders believe you," said Miss Rachel. "Another cookie?"

They helped themselves, said goodbye to Miss Rachel, and continued on their way, munching on cookies and still talking about the wondrous thing that had just happened. The day could hardly get better, they decided, but they were still on the search for adventure. It was just that sort of day.

They spent an hour playing in the Lot with a few other boys and had a grand game of pirates before they all parted for lunch. Arthur found his lunch sitting out in the kitchen with a note attached. Lydia said she was very tired and was taking a nap with Alice. Arthur ate his lunch and went out to find Kip again. Kip was just finishing his lunch. Mrs. Mortimer gave them each a cookie and sent them out to play. She was going to mop the kitchen floor, and she could not have them underfoot.

"Let's go in the grove," Arthur suggested. So they went to the grove, and immediately became bandits hiding amongst the trees. The bandits robbed and pillaged and wreaked havoc until they decided they were hungry again, and went in search of food.

On the way back to the Mortimers' they came across a man. He was sitting against a tree, and his eyes were closed. He was a very scruffy-looking man. He looked like Mr. Mortimer and Dennis looked in the morning before they had shaved, only worse. He was holding a strange-looking bundle wrapped in blue in his arms. He seemed to be asleep, so they crept away.

"Who do you think he is?" Arthur whispered as they crept away.

"I don't know," Kip whispered back. "I've never seen him before."

"He looks like a bandit," Arthur said.

"He does," Kip agreed. "I bet he's a real live bandit."

When they reached Kip's house they found the whole street in havoc. There was a big group of people around the Ramsays' house. The boys squeezed through and found Lydia and Dennis there. Lydia was sobbing, and Dennis was holding her in his arms.

"What's the matter?" Arthur asked.

Dennis turned to him. "Arthur. Somebody took Alice."

Arthur gasped. "Who? What happened?"

"I had her in her carriage, and we were going to take a walk," Lydia sobbed. "I left her on the porch for a minute while I went to answer the telephone, and when I came back she was gone. I didn't think anyone would take her. I've left her on the porch many times, and nothing's happened."

"Who would take Alice?" Arthur asked.

"Someone very bad," Dennis said. "We've called the police. They'll be here any minute."

Kip tugged on Arthur's arm. "Arthur," he whispered, "I have an idea!"

Arthur followed him away from the group of people. "What is it?"

"That man in the grove," Kip said excitedly. "He had that funny-looking bundle that was all blue. Doesn't Alice have a blue blanket?"

Arthur nodded, and suddenly became very excited. "Yes! He must be the one who took her! Kip! Maybe he's still asleep. If he is, maybe we can take Alice and run as fast as we can before he can catch us."

Kip nodded. "If he sees the police, he might run away, and then we'd never get her back."

The thought was not a pleasant one. "Let's go right now," Arthur said. They made sure no one was watching them, and slipped off into the grove.

The man was still there, and he still seemed to be asleep. The boys looked at each other, and after Arthur had counted down from three on his fingers, they ran softly up to him. Arthur pulled on the bundle.

The man's eyes flew open. He jumped up, clutching the bundle to him. "We can't let him get away!" Arthur cried.

Kip rose to the occasion. With a flying leap he grabbed the man around his legs and held on as hard as he could. Arthur followed and grabbed him from behind. The man struggled, but with a baby in his arms and two boys hanging onto him, there was little he could do.

"You can't have our baby!" Arthur yelled at him.

"Give her back!" Kip cried.

The man suddenly sat down with a grunt of pain. To their surprise, Arthur and Kip saw that he was crying. They had never seen a grown man cry before. "I didn't mean to take her," the man sobbed. "I mean, I did mean to take her, but I was going to give her back. I just wanted to hold her for a minute, but then I heard someone coming, and I panicked and ran, and I didn't even realize I still had the baby. I was going to put her back when I realized I was still holding her, but there were so many people around the house, and I heard someone say they were calling the police."

Arthur sat down on the man's legs and looked at him in puzzlement. "Why did you want to hold Alice?" he asked.

"Is that her name?" The man opened the blanket a little and touched Alice's face gently with one of his big, dirty fingers. "It's a pretty name."

"But why did you want to hold her?" Arthur demanded again.

The man sighed. "I haven't eaten or slept for days. I suppose I was kind of losing it, and when I saw your baby I thought that she was my own little girl, and I just had to hold her for a minute. She's so pretty." He smiled down at Alice and touched her face again with his finger.

"Where's your baby?" Kip asked.

"She's at an orphan home," the man said. "My wife died, and I was fired from my job because I hurt my arm, so they took my little girl. I've been looking for work so I can get my Joan back, but no one wants to hire me, because of my arm. I came here to look for an old friend, but now I don't think that's such a good idea. They'll be on the lookout for me." He sighed again. "I don't know what to do. I just want my little girl."

Kip jumped up. "I know!" he cried. "Maybe my father can get you some work. He knows lots of people in town. "Why don't we go ask him?"

The man shook his head. "The police will be there. They'll just arrest me, and I'll never get my little girl back."

This did seem to be a dilemma. The boys thought hard about it, and finally Arthur came up with a plan. "Why don't you give us Alice," he said, "and I can bring her back. Kip can stay with you, and I'll tell Dennis and Lydia about you and ask them not to arrest you, and I'll ask Kip's father if he can find you some work so you can get your baby back."

The man smiled a little. "I don't think they'll stop from arresting me just because you ask them to."

Arthur thought about this. "I have an idea. We can hide you, and tell them we won't let them know where you are until they promise not to arrest you."

The man shrugged. "Well, I suppose it's worth a try. I'm at my wit's end as it is."

"Right," said Arthur. "Kip, why don't you take him to our bandits' lair, and I'll go back with Alice." He turned to the man. "Promise you won't run away?"

The man nodded. "I promise."

"Good. And I promise I'll make sure they don't arrest you," Arthur said.

"Thank you," said the man. He held out his hand, and Arthur shook it. The man gave him Alice, and Arthur carefully carried her back to the house.

The police had arrived by that time, and they were questioning Lydia. But everyone stopped what they were doing and stared at Arthur as he approached with Alice in his arms. Lydia gave a cry and ran towards him, with Dennis close behind. "My baby! My baby!" Lydia kept crying as she snatched Alice up and held her tightly.

"Arthur! Where did you find her?" Dennis asked. Arthur explained what had happened. Everyone listened in silence. When Arthur had finished, there was another long silence. Finally Dennis said, "He ought to be put in jail!"

"No!" Arthur cried. "You can't do that. We promised him. Please, you have to help him."

Lydia had been looking at him in a peculiar way. Now she said slowly, "I think Arthur's right. We should at least talk to the man."

"Lydia, he stole our baby," Dennis said.

"I know," said Lydia. "But if he's telling the truth, and he might never see his little girl again, I feel so sorry for him. Please, Dennis. We have our baby back. Why don't we help this man get his baby back?"

Dennis kissed her. "You are always so kind to everyone. Very well, let's meet this man and see what he has to say. Where is he, Arthur?"

"He's hiding with Kip," Arthur said. "I'll go get him." He ran off and found Kip and the man still in the bandits' lair. Breathlessly he told them that Dennis and Lydia had agreed to meet him and help him if they could.

Everyone was silent as Arthur and Kip came back with the man. The three of them went up to the Ramsays' front porch. Most of the police had gone, and only two remained, just in case.

Suddenly the man stopped and stared hard. He was looking straight at Mr. Mortimer. "Henry Mortimer?" he said.

Mr. Mortimer stared back. Suddenly he burst into a laugh and hurried up to the man. "James Blake!" he cried, and shook the man's hand hard. "I haven't seen you in years. What brings you here?" He stopped and a sad look came over his face. "Is it true what Arthur told us?"

The man nodded. "I wish it wasn't. I came here to find you." He smiled a little. "I didn't expect to find you under these circumstances."

"Well, everyone," Mr. Mortimer said, turning around, "the mystery's solved. This is my old friend, James Blake."

There was instantly a lot of grown-up talk. Arthur and Kip were forgotten. They sat down on the porch steps and watched the grownups as they chattered. The policemen left, and one by one the neighbors left.

Miss Rachel stopped in front of the boys. "Well," she said, "it seems that you two are quite the heroes today. Well done, boys!" She smiled at them and left.

When everyone was gone except for the Ramsays and the Mortimers and Mr. Mortimer's friend Mr. Blake, Arthur decided he had had enough of grownup chatter, and he announced, "I'm hungry."

Everyone's attention was instantly turned to the boys. Lydia hugged them and thanked them. Mr. Mortimer shook their hands and said, "Dennis, I believe we have two boys that we can be very proud of. I think they deserve a special treat, don't you?"

Dennis smiled. "I certainly do. Well done, boys."

"How about dinner to celebrate?" Mrs. Mortimer suggested. "I'll make a chocolate cake."

When the grownups and baby Alice had gone inside to begin their dinner preparations, Arthur and Kip remained outside on the porch steps. They sat side by side, silent, happy, and contented. It had been an eventful day, but a very good day, the kind of day they dreamed about, but didn't think would actually happen. They had set out in search of adventure, and had met with a real one. It was the stuff of books, not the stuff of everyday life. But sometimes everyday life could surprise a person. They looked at each other and smiled happily. The summer was off to a very good start.

www.ingramcontent.com/pod-product-compliance
Lightning Source LLC
Chambersburg PA
CBHW030342030726
47499CB00003B/870